STINGAREE

Stingaree is a master of disguises. In Australia, he pretends to be the renowned British composer, Sir Julian Kent, visiting the wealthy Mr and Mrs Hugh Clarkson's house. There, he meets Hilda Bouverie, a lowly servant girl, who dreams of being an opera singer. However, Stingaree is discovered as being an impostor and he escapes with Hilda to his hideout, where he realises that he loves her. When the genuine Sir Julian eventually hears Hilda sing, it results in his inviting her to come to England. Meanwhile Stingaree's exploits lead to a shooting and his arrest . . .

Books by E. W. Hornung
Published by The House of Ulverscroft:

THE BLACK MASK
A THIEF IN THE NIGHT
MR JUSTICE RAFFLES

E. W. HORNUNG

STINGAREE

Complete and Unabridged

ULVERSCROFT
Leicester

First published in Great Britain in 1905

This Large Print Edition
published 2013

The moral right of the author has been asserted

A catalogue record for this book is available
from the British Library.

ISBN 978–1–4448–1605–1

Published by
F. A. Thorpe (Publishing)
Anstey, Leicestershire

Set by Words & Graphics Ltd.
Anstey, Leicestershire
Printed and bound in Great Britain by
T. J. International Ltd., Padstow, Cornwall

This book is printed on acid-free paper

A Voice in the Wilderness

I

'La parlate d'amor,
O cari fior,
Recate i miei sospiri,
Narrate i miei matiri,
Ditele o cari fior — '

Miss Bouverie ceased on the high note, as abruptly as string that snaps beneath the bow, and revolved with the music-stool, to catch but her echoes in the empty room. None had entered behind her back; there was neither sound nor shadow in the deep veranda through the open door. But for the startled girl at the open piano, Mrs. Clarkson's sanctum was precisely as Mrs. Clarkson had left it an hour before; her own photograph, in as many modes, beamed from the usual number of ornamental frames; there was nothing whatever to confirm a wild suspicion of the living lady's untimely return. And yet either guilty conscience, or an ear as sensitive as it was true, had heard an unmistakable step outside.

1

Hilda Bouverie lived to look magnificent when she sang, her fine frame drawn up to its last inch, her throat a pillar of pale coral, her mouth the perfect round, her teeth a noble relic of barbarism; but sweeter she never was than in these days, or at this moment of them, as she sat with lips just parted and teeth just showing, in a simple summer frock of her own unaided making. Her eyes, of the one deep Tasmanian blue, were still open very wide, but no longer with the same apprehension; for a step there was, but a step that jingled; nor did they recognize the silhouette in top-boots which at length stood bowing on the threshold.

'Please finish it!' prayed a voice that Miss Bouverie liked in her turn; but it was too much at ease for one entirely strange to her, and she rose with little embarrassment and no hesitation at all.

'Indeed, no! I thought I had the station to myself.'

'So you had — I have not seen a soul.'

Miss Bouverie instantly perceived that honors were due from her.

'I am so sorry! You've come to see Mr. and Mrs. Clarkson?' she cried. 'Mrs. Clarkson has just left for Melbourne with her maid, and Mr. Clarkson has gone mustering with all his men. But the Indian cook is about somewhere. I'll find him, and he shall make some tea.'

The visitor planted himself with much gallantry in the doorway; he was a man still young, with a single eye-glass and a martial mustache, which combined to give distinction to a somewhat swarthy countenance. At the moment he had also an engaging smile.

'I didn't come to see either Mr. or Mrs. Clarkson,' said he; 'in fact, I never heard their name before. I was passing the station, and I simply came to see who it was who could sing like that — to believe my own ears!'

Miss Bouverie was thrilled. The stranger spoke with an authority that she divined, a sincerity which she instinctively took on trust. Her breath came quickly; she was a little nervous now.

'If you won't sing to my face,' he went on, 'I must go back to where I hung up my horse, and pray that you will at least send me on my way rejoicing. You will do that in any case. I didn't know there was such a voice in these parts. You sing a good deal, of course?'

'I haven't sung for months.'

He was now in the room; there was no longer any necessity to bar the doorway, and the light coming through fell full on his amazement. The girl stood before him with a calm face, more wistful than ironic, yet with hints of humor in the dark blue eyes. Her companion put up the eye-glass which he had dropped at her reply.

'May I ask what you are doing in these wilds?'

'Certainly. I am Mrs. Clarkson's companion.'

'And you sing, for the first time in months, the minute her back is turned: has the lady no soul for music?'

'You had better ask the lady.'

And her visible humor reached the corners of Miss Bouverie's mouth.

'She sings herself, perhaps?'

'And I am here to play her accompaniments!'

The eye-glass focussed the great, smiling girl.

'*Can* she sing?'

'She has a voice.'

'But have you never let her hear yours?'

'Once. I had not been here long enough to know better. And I made my usual mistake.'

'What is that?'

'I thought I had the station to myself.'

The questioner bowed to his rebuke. 'Well?' he persisted none the less.

'I was told exactly what my voice was like, and fit for.'

The gentleman turned on his heel, as though her appreciation of the humor of her position were an annoyance to him. His movement brought him face to face with a photographic galaxy of ladies in varying styles of evening dress, with an equal variety in coiffures, but a certain family likeness running through the series.

'Are any of these Mrs. Clarkson?'

'All of them.'

He muttered something in his mustache. 'And what's this?' he asked of a sudden.

The young man (for as such Miss Bouverie was beginning to regard him) was standing under the flaming bill of a grand concert to be given in the township of Yallarook for the benefit of local charities.

'Oh, that's Mrs. Clarkson's concert,' he was informed. 'She has been getting it up, and that's why she's had to go to Melbourne — about her dress, you know.'

He smiled sardonically through mustache and monocle.

'Her charity begins near home!'

'It need not necessarily end there.'

'Yet she sings five times herself.'

'True — without the encores.'

'And you don't sing at all.'

'But I accompany.'

'A bitter irony! But, I say, what's this?

'Under the distinguished patronage of Sir Julian Crum, Mus. Doc., D.C.L.' Who may he be?'

'Director of the Royal College of Music, in the old country,' the girl answered with a sigh.

'Royal College of Music? That's something new, since my time,' said the visitor, sighing also. 'But what's a man like that doing out here?'

'He has a brother a squatter, the next station but one. Sir Julian's spending the English winter with him on account of his health.'

'So you've seen something of him?'

'I wish we had.'

'But Mrs. Clarkson has?'

'No — not yet.'

'I see!' and an enlightened gleam shot through the eye-glass. 'So this is her way of getting to know a poor overworked wreck who came out to patch his lungs in peace and quiet! And she's going to sing him one of his own songs; she's gone to Melbourne to dress the part; and you're not going to sing anything at all!'

Miss Bouverie refrained alike from comment and confirmation; but her silence was the less creditable in that her companion was now communing chiefly with himself. She

6

felt, indeed, that she had already been guilty of a certain disloyalty to one to whom she owed some manner of allegiance; but that was the extent of Miss Bouverie's indiscretion in her own eyes. It caused her no qualms to entertain an anonymous gentleman whom she had never seen before. A colder course had commended itself to the young lady fresh from London; but to a Colonial girl, on a station where special provision was made for the entertaining of strange travellers, the situation was simply conventional. It might have been less onerous with host or hostess on the spot; but then the visitor would not have heard her sing, and he seemed to know what singing was.

Miss Bouverie watched him as he leant over the piano, looking through the songs which she had dared once more to bring forth from her room. She might well have taken a romantic interest in the dark and dapper man, with the military eye-glass and mustache, the spruce duck jacket and the spurred top-boots. It was her first meeting with such a type in the back-blocks of New South Wales. The gallant ease, the natural gayety, the charming manners that charmed no less for a clear trace of mannerism, were a peculiar refreshment after society racier of Riverina soil. Yet it was none of these things which attracted this woman to this man; for the susceptible girl was dead in her for the time being; but the desperate artist was alive again after many weeks, was panting for fresh life, was catching at a straw. He had heard her sing. It had brought him galloping off the track. He praised her voice; and he knew — he knew what singing was.

Who could he be? Not . . . could that be possible?

'Sing me this,' he said, suddenly, and, seating himself at the piano, played the opening bars of a vocal adaptation of Handel's Largo with a just, though unpractised, touch.

Nothing could have afforded a finer hearing of the quality and the compass of her voice, and she knew of old how well it suited her; yet at the outset, from the sheer excitement of her suspicion, Hilda Bouverie was shaky to the point of a pronounced tremolo. It wore off with the lengthening cadences, and in a minute the little building was bursting with her voice, while the pianist swayed and bent upon his stool with the exuberant sympathy of a brother in art. And when the last rich note had died away he wheeled about, and so sat silent for many moments, looking curiously on her flushed face and panting bosom.

'I can't place your voice,' he said, at last. 'It's both voices — the most wonderful compass in the world — and the world will tell you so, when you go back to it, as go back you must and shall. May I ask the name of your master?'

'My own name — Bouverie. It was my father. He is dead.'

Her eyes glistened.

'You did not go to another?'

'I had no money. Besides, he had lived for what you say; when he died with his dream still a dream, I said I would do the same, and I came up here.'

She had turned away. A less tactful interlocutor had sought plainer repudiation of the rash resolve; this one rose and buried himself in more songs.

'I have heard you in Grand Opera, and in something really grand,' he said. 'Now I want a song, the simpler the better.'

Behind his back a daring light came into the moist eyes.

'There is one of Mrs. Clarkson's,' she said. 'She would never forgive me for singing it, but I have heard it from her so often, I know so well how it ought to go.'

And, fetching the song from a cabinet, she thrust it boldly under his nose. It was called 'The Unrealized Ideal,' and was a setting of some words by a real poet then living, whose name caused this reader to murmur, 'London Lyrics!' The composer was Sir Julian Crum. But his name was read without a word, or a movement of the strong shoulders and the tanned neck on which Miss Bouverie's eyes were fixed.

'You had better play this yourself,' said he, after peering at the music through his glass. 'It is rather too many for me.'

And, strangely crestfallen, Miss Bouverie took his place.

'My only love is always near,
    In country or in town:
I see her twinkling feet, I hear
    The whisper of her gown.

'She foots it, ever fair and young,
    Her locks are tied in haste,
And one is o'er her shoulder flung
    And hangs below her waist.'

For that was the immortal trifle. How much of its immortality it will owe to the setting of Sir Julian Crum is a matter of opinion, but here is an anonymous view.

'I like the words, Miss Bouverie, but the setting doesn't take me. It might with repetition. It seems lacking in go and simplicity; technically, I should say, a gem. But there can be no two opinions of your singing of such a song; that's the sort of arrow to go straight to the heart of the public — a world-wide public — and if I am the first to say it to you, I hope you will one day remember it in my favor. Meanwhile it is for me to thank you — from my heart — and to say good-by!'

He was holding out a sunburnt hand.

'Must you go?' she asked, withholding her own in frank disappointment.

'Unfortunately, yes; my man is waiting for me with both horses in the scrub. But before I go I want to ask a great favor of you. It is — not to tell a soul I have been here.'

For a singer and a woman of temperament, Hilda Bouverie had a wonderfully level head. She inquired his reason in no promising tone.

'You will see at Mrs. Clarkson's concert.'

Hilda started.

'You are coming to that?'

'Without fail — to hear Mrs. Clarkson sing five songs — your song among them!'

'But it's hers; it has been the other way about.'

The gay smile broadened on the swarthy face; a very bright eye twinkled through the monocle into those of Miss Bouverie.

'Well, will you promise to say nothing

about me? I have a reason which you will be the first to appreciate in due season.'

Hilda hesitated, reasoned with herself, and finally gave her word. Their hands were joined an instant, as he thanked her with gallant smile and bow. Then he was gone. And as his spurs ceased jingling on the veranda outside, Hilda Bouverie glanced again at the song on the piano and clapped her hands with unreasonable pride.

'I do believe that I was right after all!' said she.

II

Mr. Clarkson and his young men sat at meat that evening with a Miss Bouverie hard to recognize as the apparently austere spinster who had hitherto been something of a skeleton at their board. Coldly handsome at her worst, a single day had brought her forth a radiant beauty wreathed in human smiles. Her clear skin had a tinge which at once suggested and dismissed the thought of rouge; but beyond all doubt she had done her hair with less reserve; and it was coppery hair of a volatile sort, that sprang into natural curls at the first relaxation of an undue discipline. Mr. Clarkson wondered whether

12

his wife's departure had aught to do with the striking change in her companion; the two young men rested mutually assured that it had.

'The old girl keeps too close an eye on her,' said little Mr. Hack, who kept the books and hailed from Middlesex. 'Get her to yourself, Ted, and she's as larky as they're made.'

Ted Radford, the station overseer, was a personage not to be dismissed in a relative clause. He was a typical back-blocker, dry and wiry, nasally cocksure, insolently cool, a fearless hand with horse, man, or woman. He was a good friend to Hack when there was no third person of his own kidney to appreciate the overseer's conception of friendly chaff. They were by themselves now, yet the last speech drew from Radford a sufficiently sardonic grin.

'You see if she is, old man,' said he, 'and I'll stand by to collect your remains. Not but what she hasn't come off the ice, and looks like thoring if you take her the right way.'

Ted Radford was a confirmed believer in the rightness of his own way with all mankind; his admirable confidence had not been shaken by a long succession of snubs in the quarter under discussion. As for Miss Bouverie, it was her practice to play off one young man against the other by discouraging each in his turn. But this evening she was a different being. She had a vague yet absolute conviction that her fortune was made. She could have sung all her songs to the twain, but for the reflection that Mr. Clarkson himself would hear them too, and report the matter to his wife on her return.

And the next night the male trio were strangely absorbed in some station happening which did not arouse Miss Bouverie's curiosity in the least. They were excited and yet constrained at dinner, and drew their chairs close together on the veranda afterward. The young lady caught at least one word of which she did not know the meaning. She had the tact to keep out of earshot after that. Nor was she very much more interested when she met the two young men with revolvers in their hands the following day.

'Going to fight a duel?' she inquired, smilingly, for her heart was still singing Grand Opera and Oratorio by turns.

'More or less,' returned the overseer, without his usual pleasantry. 'We're going to have a match at a target behind the pines.'

The London bookkeeper looked an anxious clerk: the girl was glad when she saw the pair alive at dinner. There seemed to be little doing. Though the summer was already tropical, there had been plenteous rains, and

Mr. Clarkson observed in Hilda's hearing that the recent day's mustering would be the last for some little time. She was thrown much in his company, and she liked Mr. Clarkson when Mrs. Clarkson was not there. In his wife's hands the good man was wax; now a mere echo, now a veritable claque in himself, he pandered indefatigably to the multitudinous vanities of a ludicrously vain woman. But it was soon Miss Bouverie's experience that he could, when he dared, be attentively considerate of lesser ladies. And in many ways these were much the happiest days that she had spent on the station.

They were, however, days of a consuming excitement for the caged and gagged nightingale that Hilda Bouverie now conceived herself to be. She sang not another note aloud. Mr. Clarkson lived in slippers on the veranda, which Hilda now associated chiefly with a stranger's spurs: for of the booted and spurred stranger she was thinking incessantly, though still without the emotions of an ordinarily romantic temperament. Would he be at the concert, or would he not? Would he turn out to be what she firmly imagined him, or was she to find out her mistake? Might he not in any case have said or written some pregnant word for her? Was it beyond the bounds of possibility that she should be asked to sing after all?

The last question was the only one to be answered before the time, unless a point-blank inquiry of Mrs. Clarkson be included in the category. The lady had returned with a gorgeous gown, only less full of her experiences than of the crowning triumph yet to come. She had bought every song of Sir Julian's to be had in Melbourne, and his name was always on her lips. In a reckless moment Miss Bouverie had inquired his age.

'I really don't know,' said Mrs. Clarkson. 'What *can* it matter?'

'I only wondered whether he was a youngish man or not.'

Mrs. Clarkson had already raised her eyebrows; at this answer they disappeared behind a *toupet* dating from her late descent upon the Victorian capital.

'Really, Miss Bouverie!' she said, and nothing more in words. But the tone was intolerable, and its accompanying sneer a refinement in vulgarity, which only the really refined would have resented as it deserved. Miss Bouverie got up and left the room without a word. But her flaming face left a misleading tale behind.

She was not introduced to Sir Julian; but that was not her prime disappointment when the great night came. All desire for an introduction, all interest in the concert, died a sudden death in Hilda Bouverie at her first glimpse of the gentleman who was duly presented to Mrs. Clarkson as Sir Julian Crum. He was more than middle-aged; he wore a gray beard, and the air of a somewhat supercilious martyr; his near sight was obviated by double lenses in gold rims. Hilda could have wept before the world. For nearly three weeks she had been bowing in imagination to a very different Sir Julian, bowing as though she had never beheld him in her life before; and yet in three minutes she saw how little real reason she had ever had for the illogical conclusion to which she had jumped. She searched for the sprightly figure she had worn in her mind's eye; his presence under any other name would still have been welcome enough now. But he was not there at all. In the patchy glare of the kerosene lamps, against the bunting which lined the corrugated walls of Gulland's new iron store, among flower and weed of township and of station, did Miss Bouverie seek in vain for a single eye-glass and a military mustache.

The concert began. Miss Bouverie opened it herself with the inevitably thankless pianoforte solo, in this case gratuitously meretricious into the bargain, albeit the arbitrary choice of no less a judge than Mrs.

17

Clarkson. It was received with perfunctory applause, through which a dissipated stockman thundered thickly for a song. Miss Bouverie averted her eyes from Sir Julian (ensconced like Royalty in the centre of the first row) as she descended from the platform. She had not the hardihood to glance toward the great man until the indistinct stockman had had his wish, and Mrs. Clarkson, in her fine new raiment, had both sung and acted a coy ditty of the previous decade, wherein every line began with the word 'somebody.' It was an immediate success; the obstreperous stockman led the encore; but Miss Bouverie, who duly accompanied, extracted solace from the depressed attitude in which Sir Julian Crum sat looking down his nose.

The township boasted its score of dwellings, but few of them showed a light that evening; not less than ninety of the round hundred of inhabitants clapped their hands and mopped their foreheads in Gulland's new store. It might have been run up for its present purpose. There was an entrance at one end for the performers, and that on the platform level, since the ground sloped a little; at the other end was the only other entrance, by which the audience were admitted. A makeshift lobby had been arranged behind the platform, and thither Mrs. Clarkson retired to await her earlier encores; when the compliment became a recognized matter of course, she abandoned the mere form of a momentary retirement, and stood patiently smiling in the satin ball-dress brought from Melbourne for the nonce. And for the brief intervals between her efforts she descended to a throne specially reserved on the great musician's right.

The other performers did not dim her brilliance by reason of their own. There was her own dear husband, whose serious recitation was the one entertaining number. There was a Rabbit Inspector who rapped out 'The Scout' in a defiant baritone, and a publican whose somewhat uneven tenor was shaken to its depths by the simple pathos of 'When Sparrows Build.' Mrs. Clarkson could afford to encourage such tyros with marked applause. The only danger was that Sir Julian might think she really admired their untutored attempts.

'One must do it,' she therefore took occasion to explain as she clapped. 'They are so nervous. The hard thing is to put oneself in their place; it's nothing to me to sing a song, Sir Julian.'

'So I can see, madam,' said he.

At the extreme end of the same row Miss

Bouverie passed her unemployed moments between Mr. Radford and the wall, and was not easy until she had signalled to little Mr. Hack to occupy the seat behind her. With the two together she felt comparatively comfortable. Mr. Radford's running criticism on the performers, always pungent, was often amusing, while Mr. Hack lost no opportunity of advancing his own ideals in the matter of musical entertainment.

'A song and dance,' said he, again and again, with a more and more sepulchral deviltry — 'a song and dance is what you want. You should have heard the Sisters Belton in their palmy days at the Pav! You don't get the best of everything out here, you know, Ted!'

'No; let's hope they've got some better men than you,' returned Radford, inspired by the quorum of three to make mince-meat of his friend.

It was the interval between parts one and two. The platform was unoccupied. A cool draught blew through the iron building from open door to open door; there was no occasion to go outside. They had done so, however, at the lower end; there was a sudden stampede of returning feet. A something in the scuffling steps, a certain outcry that accompanied them, caused Miss Bouverie and her companions to turn their heads; they turned again at as sudden a jingle on the platform, and the girl caught her breath. There stood her missing hero, smiling on the people, dapper, swarthy, booted, spurred, and for one moment the man she had reason to remember, exactly as she remembered him. The next his folded arms sprang out from the shoulders, and a brace of long-barrelled revolvers covered the assembly.

'Up with your hands, every man of you!' he cried. 'No, not the ladies, but every man and boy who doesn't want a bullet in his brain!'

The command was echoed in uncouth accents at the lower door, where, in fact, a bearded savage had driven in all and sundry at his pistol's point. And in a few seconds the meeting was one which had carried by overwhelming show of hands a proposition from which the ladies alone saw occasion to dissent.

'You may have heard of me before,' said the man on the platform, sweeping the forest of hands with his eye-glass. 'My name's Stingaree.'

It was the word which Hilda Bouverie had heard on the veranda and taken for some strange expletive.

'Who is he?' she asked, in a whisper that bespoke excitement, agitation, but not alarm.

21

'The fancy bushranger — the dandy outlaw!' drawled Radford, in cool reply. 'I've been expecting him. He was seen on our run the day Mrs. Clarkson went down to Melbourne.'

That memorable day for Hilda Bouverie! And it was this manner of man who had been her hero ever since: a bushranger, an outlaw, a common robber under arms!

'And you never told me!' she cried, in an indignant whisper.

'We never told Mrs. Clarkson either. You must blame the boss.'

Hilda snatched her eyes from Stingaree, and was sorry for Mrs. Clarkson for the first time in their acquaintance. The new ball-dress of bridal satin was no whiter than its wearer's face, which had aged several years in as many seconds. The squatter leant toward her with uplifted hands, loyally concerned for no one and for nothing else. Between the couple Sir Julian might have been conducting without his bâton, but with both arms. Meanwhile, the flashing eye-glass had fixed itself on Miss Bouverie's companion, without resting for an instant on Miss Bouverie.

'Silence over there!' cried Stingaree, sternly. 'I'm here on a perfectly harmless errand. If you know anything about me at all, you may know that I have a weakness for music of any kind, so long as it's good of its kind.'

The eye-glass dropped for a moment upon Mrs. Clarkson in the front row, and the irrepressible Radford was enabled to continue his say.

'He has, too, from a mouth-organ to a full orchestra, from all accounts, Miss Bouverie. *My revolver's in the coat-pocket next you!*'

'It is the music,' continued Stingaree, looking harder than before in their direction, 'which has brought me here to-night. I've come to listen, and for no other reason in the world. Unfortunately, when one has a price upon one's head, one has to take certain precautions before venturing among one's fellow-men. And, though I'm not here for gain or bloodshed, if any man of you gives me trouble I shall shoot him like a dog!'

'That's one for me,' whispered the intrepid overseer, in lower key. 'Never mind. He's not looking at us now. I believe Mrs. Clarkson's going to faint. *You take what I told you and slip it under your shawl, and you'll save a second by passing it up to me the instant you see her sway!*'

Hilda hesitated. A dead silence had fallen on the crowded and heated store, and in the silence Stingaree was already taking an unguarded interest in Mrs. Clarkson's appearance, which as certainly betokened imminent collapse. 'Now!' whispered Radford, and Hilda hesitated no more. She was wearing a black lace shawl between her appearances at the piano; she had the revolver under it in a twinkling, and pressed it to her bosom with both hands, one outside the shawl and one underneath, as who should hug a beating heart.

'Mrs. Clarkson,' said Stingaree, 'you have been singing too much, and the quality of your song has not been equal to the quantity.'

It sounded a brutal speech enough; and to do justice to a portion of the audience not hitherto remarkable for its spirit, the ungallant criticism was audibly resented in the back rows. The maudlin stockman had indeed to be restrained by his neighbors from precipitating himself upon the barrels of Stingaree. But the effect upon Mrs. Clarkson herself was still more remarkable, and revealed a subtle kindness in the desperado's cruelty. Her pale face flushed; her lack-lustre eyes blazed forth their indignation; her very clay was on fire for all the room to see.

'I don't sing for criminals and cut-throats!' the indignant lady cried out. She glanced at Sir Julian as one for whom she did sing. And Sir Julian's eyes twinkled under the bushranger's guns.

'To be sure you don't,' said Stingaree, with

as much sweetness as his character would permit. 'You sing for charity, and spend three times as much as you are ever likely to make in arraying yourself for the occasion. Well, we must put up with some song-bird without fine feathers, for I mean to hear the programme out.' His eyes ranged the front rows till they fell on Hilda Bouverie in her corner. 'You young lady over there! You've been talking since I called for silence. You deserve to pay a penalty; be good enough to step this way.'

Hilda's excitement may be supposed; it made her scandalously radiant in that company of humiliated men and women, but it did not rob her of her resource. Removing her shawl with apparent haste, but with calculated deliberation, she laid it in a bunch upon the seat which she had occupied, and stepped forward with a courage that won a cheer from the back rows. Stingaree stooped to hand her up to the platform; and his warm grip told a tale. This was what he had come for, to make her sing, to make her sing before Sir Julian Crum, to give her a start unique in the history of the platform and the stage. Criminal, was he? Then the dearest, kindest, most enchanting, most romantic criminal the world had ever seen! But she must be worthy of his chivalry and her chance; and, from the first, her artistic egoism insisted that she was.

Stingaree had picked up a programme, and dexterously mounted it between hammer and cartridge of the revolver which he had momentarily relinquished, much as a cornet-player mounts his music under his nose. With both weapons once more levelled, he consulted the programme now.

'The next item, ladies and gentlemen,' said he, 'is another pianoforte solo by this young lady. We'll let you off that, Miss Bouverie, since you've got to sing. The next song on the programme is called 'The Unrealized Ideal,' and the music is by our distinguished visitor and patron, Sir Julian Crum. In happier circumstances it would have been sung to you by Mrs. Montgomery Clarkson; as it is, I call upon Miss Bouverie to realize her ideal and ours, and on Sir Julian Crum to accompany her, if he will.'

At Mrs. Clarkson's stony side the great man dropped both arms at the superb impudence of the invitation.

'Quite right, Sir Julian; let the blood run into them,' said Stingaree. 'It is a pure oversight that you were not exempted in the beginning. Comply with my entreaty and I guarantee that you shall suffer no further inconvenience.'

Sir Julian wavered. In London he was a

club-man and a diner-out; and what a tale for the Athenæum — what a short cut to every ear at a Kensington dinner-table! In the end it would get into the papers. That was the worst of it. But in the midst of Sir Julian's hesitation his pondering eyes met those of Miss Bouverie — on fire to sing him his own song — alight with the ability to do it justice. And Sir Julian was lost.

How she sang it may be guessed. Sir Julian bowed and swayed upon his stool. Stingaree stood by with a smile of personal pride and responsibility, but with both revolvers still levelled, and one of them cocked. It was a better song than he had supposed. It gained enormously from the composer's accompaniment. The last verse was softer than another would have made it, and yet the singer obeyed inaudible instructions as though she had never sung it otherwise. It was more in a tuneful whisper than in hushed notes that the last words left her lips: —

'Lightly I sped when hope was high,
    And youth beguiled the chase;
I follow — follow still; but I
    Shall never see her Face.'

The applause, when it came, was almost overwhelming. The bushranger watched and

27

smiled, but cocked his second pistol, and let the programme flutter to the floor. As for Sir Julian Crum, the self-contained, the cynical, he was seen for an instant, wheeled about on the music-stool, grasping the singer by both hands. But there was no hearing what he said; the girl herself heard nothing until he bellowed in her ear:

'They'll have their encore. What can you give them? It must be something they know. 'Home, Sweet Home'? 'The Last Rose'? 'Within a Mile'? The first, eh? Very well; it's a leaf out of Patti's book; but so are they all.'

And he struck the opening bars in the key of his own song, but for some moments Hilda Bouverie stood bereft of her great voice. A leaf out of Patti's book, in that up-country township, before a roomful held in terror — and yet unmindful — of the loaded pistols of two bloodthirsty bushrangers! The singer prayed for power to live up to those golden words. A leaf out of Patti's book!

It was over. The last poignant note trembled into nothingness. The silence, absolutely dead for some seconds, was then only broken by a spirituous sob from the incorrigible stockman. There was never any applause at all. Ere it came, even as it was coming, the overseer Radford leapt to his feet with a raucous shout.

The bushranger had vanished from the platform. The other bushranger had disappeared through the other door. The precious pair of them had melted from the room unseen, unheard, what time every eye doted on handsome Hilda Bouverie, and every ear on the simple words and moving cadences of 'Home, Sweet Home.'

Ted Radford was the first to see it; for by the end of the brief song he had his revolver uncovered and cocked at last, and no quarry left for him to shoot. With a bound he was on the platform; another carried him into the canvas anteroom, a third and a fourth out into the moonlight. It was as bright as noon in a conservatory of smoked glass. And in the tinted brightness one man was already galloping away; but it was Stingaree who danced with one foot only in the stirrup of a milk-white mare.

Radford rushed up to him and fired point-blank again and again. A series of metallic clicks was all the harm he did, for Stingaree was in the saddle before the hurled revolver struck the mare on the ribs, and sent the pair flying through the moonlight with a shout of laughter, a cloud of sand, and a dull volley of thunderous hoofs. The overseer picked up his revolver and returned crestfallen to examine it in the lights of the emptying room.

'I could have sworn I loaded it,' said he. 'If I had, he'd have been a dead man six times over.'

Miss Bouverie had been talking to Sir Julian Crum. On Radford's entry she had grown *distraite*, but at Radford's speech she turned back to Sir Julian with shining eyes.

'My wife wants a companion for the voyage,' he was saying. 'So that will cost you nothing, but if anything the other way, and once in London, I'll be answerable. I've adjudicated these things for years to voices not in the same class as yours. But the worst of it is you won't stay with us.'

'I will.'

'No; they'll want you at Covent Garden before we know where we are. And when you are ready to go to them, go you must.'

'I shall do what you tell me.'

'Then speak to Mrs. Clarkson at once.'

Hilda Bouverie glanced over her shoulder, but her employers had left the building. Her smile was less roguish than demure.

'There is no need, Sir Julian. Mrs. Clarkson has already spoken to me, though only in a whisper. But I am to take myself off by the next coach.'

The Black Hole of Glenranald

It was coming up the Murrumbidgee that Fergus Carrick first heard the name of Stingaree. With the cautious enterprise of his race, the young gentleman had booked steerage on a river steamer whose solitary passenger he proved to be; accordingly he was not only permitted to sleep on the saloon settee at nights, but graciously bidden to the captain's board by day. It was there that Fergus Carrick encouraged tales of the bushrangers as the one cleanly topic familiar in the mouth of the elderly engineer who completed the party. And it seemed that the knighthood of the up-country road had been an extinct order from the extirpation of the Kellys to the appearance of this same Stingaree, who was reported a man of birth and mystery, with an ostentatious passion for music and as romantic a method as that of any highwayman of the Old World from which he hailed. But the callow Fergus had been spared the romantic temperament, and was less impressed than entertained with what he heard.

On his arrival at Glenranald, however, he

found that substantial township shaking with laughter over the outlaw's latest and least discreditable exploit, at the back-block hamlet of Yallarook; and then it was that young Carrick first conceived an ambition to open his Colonial career with the capture of Stingaree; for he was a serious immigrant, who had come out in his teens, to stay out, if necessary, for the term of his natural life.

The idea had birth under one of the many pine trees which shaded the skeleton streets of budding Glenranald. On this tree was nailed a placard offering high reward for the bushranger's person alive or dead. Fergus was making an immediate note in his pocketbook when a hand fell on his shoulder.

'Would ye like the half o' yon?' inquired a voice in his own tongue; and there at his elbow stood an elderly gentleman, whose patriarchal beard hid half the buttons of his alpaca coat, while a black skull-cap sat somewhat jauntily on his head.

'What do you mean?' said Fergus, bluntly, for the old gentleman stood chuckling gently in his venerable beard.

'To lay a hold of him,' replied the other, 'with the help o' some younger and abler-bodied man; and you're the very one I want.'

The raw youth stared ingenuously.

'But what can you know about me?'

'I saw ye land at the wharf,' said the old gentleman, nodding his approval of the question, 'and says I, 'That's my man,' as soon as ever I clapped eyes on ye. So I had a crack wi' the captain o' yon steamer; he told me you hadna a billet, but were just on the lookout for the best ye could get, an' that's all he'd been able to get out o' ye in a five days' voyage. That was enough for me. I want a man who can keep his tongue behind his teeth, and I wanted you before I knew you were a brither Scot!'

'Are you a squatter, sir?' the young man asked, a little overwhelmed.

'No, sir, I'm branch manager o' the Bank o' New South Wales, the only bank within a hunder miles o' where we stand; and I can offer ye a better billet than any squatter in the Colony.'

'Indeed? I'm sure you're very kind, sir, but I'm wanting to get on a station,' protested Fergus with all his tact. 'And as a matter of fact, I have introductions to one or two stations further back, though I saw no reason to tell our friend the skipper so.'

'Quite right, quite right! I like a man who can keep his tongue in its kennel!' cried the bank manager, rubbing his hands. 'But wait while I tell ye: ye'd need to work for your rations an any station I ever heard tell of, and I keep the accounts of enough to know. Now, with me, ye'd get two pound a week till your share o' the reward was wiped off; and if we had no luck for a year you'd be no worse off, but could go and try your squatters then. That's a promise, and I'll keep it as sure as my name's Andr' Macbean!'

'But how do you propose to catch this fellow, Mr. Macbean?'

The bank manager looked on all sides, likewise behind the tree, before replying under his breath: 'By setting a wee trap for him! A bank's a bank, and Stingaree hasna stuck one up since he took to his trade. But I'll tell ye no more till ye give me your answer. Yes or no?'

'I'm afraid I don't even write an office hand; and as for figures — '

Mr. Macbean laughed outright.

'Did I say I was going to take ye into the bank, mun?' cried he. 'There's three of us already to do the writin' an' the cipherin,' an' three's enough. Can you ride?'

'I have ridden.'

'And ye'll do any rough job I set ye to?'

'The rougher the better.'

'That's all I ask. There's a buggy and a pair for ye to mind, and mebbe drive, though it's horseback errands you'll do most of. I'm an old widower, living alone with an aged housekeeper. The cashier and the clerk dig in the township, and I need to have a man of some sort about the place; in fact, I have one, but I'll soon get rid of him if you'll come instead. Understand, you live in the house with me, just like the jackeroos on the stations; and like the jackeroos, you do all the odd jobs and dirty work that no one else'll look at; but, unlike them, you get two pounds a week from the first for doing it.'

Mr. Andrew Macbean had chanced upon a magic word. It was the position of 'jackeroo,' or utility parlor-man, on one or other of the stations to which he carried introductions, that his young countryman had set before him as his goal. True, a bank in a bush township was not a station in the bush itself. On the other hand, his would-be friend was not the first to warn Fergus against the futility of expecting more than a nominal salary as a babe and suckling in Colonial experience; and perhaps the prime elements of that experience might be gained as well in the purlieus of a sufficiently remote township as in realms unnamed on any map. It will be seen that the sober stripling was reduced to arguing with himself, and that his main argument was not to be admitted in his own heart. The mysterious eccentricity of his employer, coupled with the adventurous character of his alleged prospects, was what induced the lad to embrace both in defiance of an unimaginative hard-headedness which he aimed at rather than possessed.

With characteristic prudence he had left his baggage on board the river-steamer, and his own hands carried it piecemeal to the bank. This was a red-brick bungalow with an ample veranda, standing back from the future street that was as yet little better than a country road. The veranda commanded a long perspective of pines, but no further bricks and mortar, and but very few weather board walls. The yard behind the house was shut in by as many outbuildings as clustered about the small homesteads which Fergus had already beheld on the banks of the Murrumbidgee. The man in charge of the yard was palpably in liquor, a chronic condition from his general appearance, and Mr. Macbean discharged him on the spot with a decision which left no loophole for appeal. The woman in charge of the house adorned another plane of civilization; she was very deaf, and very outspoken on her introduction to the young gentleman, whose face she was pleased to approve, with the implied reservation that all faces were liars; but she served up the mutton of the country hot and tender; and Fergus

Carrick, leaning back after an excellent repast, marvelled for the twentieth time that he was not to pay for it.

'A teetotaler, are ye?' said Macbean, mixing a third glass of whiskey, with the skull-cap on the back of his head. 'And so was I at your age; but you're my very man. There are some it sets talking. Wait till the old lady turns in, and then you shall see what you shall see.'

Fergus waited in increasing excitement. The day's events were worthier of a dream. To have set foot in Glenranald without knowing a soul in the place, and to find one's self comfortably housed at a good salary before night! There were moments when he questioned the complete sanity of his eccentric benefactor, who drank whiskey like water, both as to quantity and effect, and who chuckled continuously in his huge gray beard. But such doubts only added to the excitement of the evening, which reached a climax when a lighted candle was thrust in at the door and the pair advised not to make a night of it by the candid crone on her way to bed.

'We will give her twenty minutes,' said the manager, winking across his glass. 'I've never let her hear me, and she mustn't hear you either. She must know nothing at all about it; nobody must, except you and me.'

The mystification of Fergus was now complete. Unimaginative as he was by practice and profession, he had an explanation a minute until the time was up, when the truth beat them all for wild improbability. Macbean had risen, lifting the lamp; holding it on high he led the way through baize doors into the banking premises. Here was another door, which Macbean not only unlocked, but locked again behind them both. A small inner office led them into a shuttered chamber of fair size, with a broad polished counter, glass swing-doors, and a formidable portal beyond. And one of young Carrick's theories received apparent confirmation on the spot; for the manager slipped behind his counter by another door, and at once whipped out a great revolver.

'This they provide us with,' said he. 'So far it is our only authorized defence, and it hangs on a hook down here behind the counter. But you march in here prepared, your pistol cocked behind your back, and which of us is likely to shoot first?'

'The bushranger,' said Fergus, still rather more startled than reassured.

'The bushranger, of course. Stingaree, let us say. As for me, either my arms go up, or down I go in a heap. But supposing my arms do go up — supposing I still touch something with one foot — and supposing the floor just opens and swallows Mr. Sanguinary Stingaree! Eh? eh? What then?'

'It would be great,' cried Fergus. 'But could it be done?'

'It can be, it will be, and is being done,' replied the manager, replacing the bank revolver and sliding over the counter like a boy. A square of plain linoleum covered the floor, overlapped by a border of the same material bearing a design. Down went Macbean upon his knees, and his beard swept this border as he began pulling it up, tacks and all.

The lamp burned brightly on the counter, its rays reflected in the burnished mahogany. All at once Fergus seized it on his own initiative, and set it on the floor before his kneeling elder, going upon his own knees on the other side. And where the plain linoleum ended, but where the overlapping border covered the floor, the planks were sawn through and through down one side of the central and self-colored square.

'A trap-door!' exclaimed Fergus in a whisper.

Macbean leant back on his slippered heels, his skull-cap wickedly awry.

'This border takes a lot o' lifting,' said he. 'Yet we've just got to lift it every time, and tack it down again before morning. You might try your hand over yonder on the far side.'

Fergus complied with so much energy that the whole border was ripped up in a minute; and he was not mistaken. A trap-door it was, of huge dimensions, almost exactly covered by the self-colored square; but at each side a tongue of linoleum had been left loose for lifting it; and the lamp had scarcely been replaced upon the counter when the bulk of the floor leaned upright in one piece against the opposite wall. It had uncovered a pit of corresponding size, but as yet hardly deep enough to afford a hiding-place for the bucket, spade, and pickaxe which lay there on a length of sacking.

'I see!' exclaimed Carrick, as the full light flooded his brain.

'Is that a fact?' inquired the manager twinkling.

'You're going to make a deep hole of it — ?'

'No. I'm going to pay you to make it deep for me — '

'And then — '

'At dead o' night; you can take out your sleep by day.'

'When Stingaree comes — '

'If he waits till we're ready for him — '

'You touch some lever — '

40

'And the floor swallows him, as I said, if he waits till we are ready for him. Everything depends on that — and on your silence. We must take time. It isn't only the digging of the hole. We need to fix up some counterpoise to make it shut after a body like a mouse-trap; we must do the thing thoroughly if we do it at all; and till it's done, not a word to a soul in the same hemisphere! In the end I suppose I shall have to tell Donkin, my cashier, and Fowler the clerk. Donkin's a disbeliever who deserves the name o' Didymus more than ony mon o' my acquaintance. Fowler would take so kindly to the whole idea that he'd blurt it out within a week. He may find it out when all's in readiness, but I'll no tell him even then. See how I trust a brither Scot at sight!'

'I much appreciate it,' said Fergus, humbly.

'I wouldna ha' trustit even you, gin I hadna found the delvin' ill worrk for auld shoulders,' pursued Macbean, broadening his speech with intentional humor. 'Noo, wull ye do't or wull ye no?'

The young man's answer was to strip off his coat and spring into the hole, and to set to work with such energy, yet so quietly, that the bucket was filled in a few almost silent seconds. Macbean carried it off, unlocking doors for the nonce, while Fergus remained in the hole to mop his forehead.

'We need to have another bucket,' said the manager, on his return. 'I've thought of every other thing. There's a disused well in the yard, and down goes every blessed bucket!'

To and fro, over the lip of the closing well, back into the throat of the deepening hole, went the buckets for many a night; and by day Fergus Carrick employed his best wits to make an intrinsically anomalous position appear natural to the world. It was a position which he himself could thoroughly enjoy; he was largely his own master. He had daily opportunities of picking up the ways and customs of the bush, and a nightly excitement which did not pall as the secret task approached conclusion; but he was subjected to much chaff and questioning from the other young bloods of Glenranald. He felt from the first that it was what he must expect. He was a groom with a place at his master's table; he was a jackeroo who introduced station life into a town. And the element of underlying mystery, really existing as it did, was detected soon enough by other young heads, led by that of Fowler, the keen bank clerk.

'I was looking at you both together, and you do favor the old man, and no error!' he would say; or else, 'What is it you could hang the boss for, Fergy, old toucher?'

These delicate but cryptic sallies being

ignored or parried, the heavy swamp of innuendo was invariably deserted for the breezy hill-top of plain speech, and Fergus had often work enough to put a guard upon hand and tongue. But his temperament was eminently self-contained, and on the whole he was an elusive target for the witticisms of his friends. There was no wit, however, and no attempt at it on the part of Donkin, the cantankerous cashier. He seldom addressed a word to Carrick, never a civil word, but more than once he treated his chief to a sarcastic remonstrance on his degrading familiarity with an underling. In such encounters the imperturbable graybeard was well able to take care of himself, albeit he expressed to Fergus a regret that he had not exercised a little more ingenuity in the beginning.

'You should have come to me with a letter of introduction,' said he.

'But who would have given me one?'

'I would, yon first night, and you'd have presented it next day in office hours,' replied the manager. 'But it's too late to think about it now, and in a few days Donkin may know the truth.'

He might have known it already, but for one difficulty. They had digged their pit to the generous depth of eight feet, so that a tall prisoner could barely touch the trap-door with extended finger-tips; and Stingaree (whose latest performance was no longer the Yallarook affair) was of medium height according to his police description. The trap-door was a double one, which parted in the centre with the deadly precision of the gallows floor. The difficulty was to make the flaps close automatically, with the mouse-trap effect of Macbean's ambition. It was managed eventually by boring separate wells for a weight behind the hinges on either side. Copper wire running on minute pulleys let into grooves suspended these weights and connected them with the flaps, and powerful door-springs supplemented the more elaborate contrivance. The lever controlling the whole was concealed under the counter, and reached by thrusting a foot through a panel, which also opened inward on a spring.

It may be conceived that all this represented the midnight labors and the constant thought of many weeks. It was now the beginning of the cool but brilliant Riverina winter, and, despite the disparity in their years, the two Scotsmen were fast friends. They had worked together as one man, with the same patient passion for perfection, the same delight in detail for its own sake. Almost the only difference was that the old fellow refreshed his energies with the glass of whiskey which was never far from his elbow after banking hours, while the young one cultivated the local excess of continual tea. And all this time the rascally Stingaree ranged the district, with or without his taciturn accomplice, covering great distances in fabulous time, lurking none knew where, and springing on the unwary in the last places in which his presence was suspected.

'But he has not yet robbed a bank, and we have our hopes,' wrote Fergus to a faithful sister at Largs. 'It may be for fear of the revolvers with which all the banks are provided now. Mr. Macbean has been practising with ours, and purposely put a bullet through one of our back windows. The whole township has been chafing him about it, and the local rag has risen to a sarcastic paragraph, which is exactly what we wanted. The trap-door over the pit is now practically finished. It's too complicated to describe, but Stingaree has only to march into the bank and 'stick it up,' and the man behind the counter has only to touch a lever with his foot for the villain to disappear through the floor into a prison it'll take him all his time to break. On Saturday the cashier and the clerk are coming to dinner, and before we sit down they are to be shown everything.'

This was but a fraction of one of the long

letters which Fergus despatched by nearly every mail. Silent and self-contained as he was, he had one confidante at the opposite end of the earth, one escape-pipe in his pen. Not a word of the great secret had he even written to another soul. To his trusted sister he had never before been quite so communicative. His conscience pricked him as he took his letter to the post, and he had it registered on no other score.

On Saturday the bank closed at one o'clock; the staff were to return and dine at seven, the Queen's birthday falling on the same day for a sufficient pretext. As the hour approached Fergus made the distressing discovery that his friend and host had anticipated the festivities with too free a hand. Macbean was not drunk, but he was perceptibly blunted and blurred, and Fergus had never seen the pale eyes so watery or the black skull-cap so much on one side of the venerable head. The lad was genuinely grieved. A whiskey bottle stood empty on the laden board, and he had the temerity to pocket the corkscrew while Macbean was gone to his storeroom for another bottle. A solemn search ensued, and then Fergus was despatched in haste for a new corkscrew.

'An' look slippy,' said Macbean, 'or we'll have old Donkin here before ye get back.'

'Not for another three-quarters of an hour,' remarked Fergus, looking at his watch.

'Any minute!' retorted Macbean, with a ribald epithet. 'I invited Donkin, in confidence, to come a good half-hour airly, and I'll tell ye for why. Donkin must ken, but I'm none so sure o' yon other impident young squirt. His tongue's too long for his mouth. Donkin or I could always be behind the counter; anyway, I mean to take his opeenion before tellin' any other body.'

Entertaining his own distrust of the vivacious Fowler, Fergus commended the decision, and so took his departure by the private entrance. It was near sundown; a fresh breeze blew along the hard road, puffing cloudlets of yellow sand into the rosy dusk. Fergus hurried till he was out of sight, and then idled shamelessly under trees. He was not going on for a new corkscrew. He was going back to confess boldly where he had found the old one. And the sight of Donkin in the distance sent him back in something of a hurry; it was quite enough to have to spend an evening with the cantankerous cashier.

The bank was practically at one end of the township as then laid out; two or three buildings there were further on, but they stood altogether aloof. The bank, for a bank, was sufficiently isolated, and Fergus could

47

not but congratulate himself on the completion of its ingenious and unsuspected defences. It only remained to keep the inventor reasonably sober for the evening, and thereafter to whistle or to pray for Stingaree. Meanwhile the present was no mean occasion, and Fergus was glad to see that Macbean had thrown open the official doors in his absence. They had often agreed that it would be worth all their labor to enlighten Donkin by letting the pit gape under his nose as he entered the bank. Fergus glanced over his shoulder, saw the other hurrying, and hurried himself in order to take up a good position for seeing the cashier's face. He was in the middle of the treacherous floor before he perceived that it was not Macbean in the half-light behind the counter, but a good-looking man whom he had never seen before.

'Didn't know I was invited, eh?' said the stranger, putting up a single eye-glass. 'Don't believe it, perhaps? You'd better ask Mr. Macbean!'

And before it had occurred to him to stir from where he stood agape, the floor fell from under the feet of Fergus, his body lurched forward, and came down flat and heavy on the hard earth eight feet below. Not entirely stunned, though shaken and hurt from head to heel, he was still collecting his senses when the pit blackened as the trap-door shut in implicit obedience to its weights and springs. And in the clinging velvet darkness the young man heard a groan.

'Is that yoursel', Fergy?'

'And are you there, Mr. Macbean?'

'Mon, didn't it shut just fine!'

Curiously blended with the physical pain in the manager's voice was a sodden philosophic humor which maddened the younger man. Fergus swore where he lay writhing on his stomach. Macbean chuckled and groaned again.

'It's Stingaree,' he said, drawing a breath through his teeth.

'Of course it is.'

'I never breathed it to a soul.'

'No more did I.'

Fergus spoke with ready confidence, and yet the words left something on his mind. It was something vague but haunting, something that made him feel instinctively unworthy of the kindly, uncomplaining tone which had annoyed him but a moment before.

'No bones broken, Fergy?'

'None that I know of.'

'I doubt I've not been so lucky. I'm thinkin' it's a rib, by the way it hurts to breathe.'

Fergus was already fumbling in his pocket. The match-box opened with a click. The match scraped several times in vain. Then at last the scene sprang out as on the screen of a magic-lantern. And to Fergus it was a very white old man, hunched up against the muddy wall, with blood upon his naked scalp and beard, and both hands pressed to his side; to the old man, a muddy face stricken with horrified concern, and a match burning down between muddy fingers; but to both, such a new view and version of their precious hole that the corners of each mouth were twitching as the match was thrown away.

Fergus was fumbling for another when a step rang overhead; and at the sharp exchange of words which both underground expected, Fergus came on all fours to the old man's side, and together they sat gazing upward into the pall of impenetrable crape.

'You infernal villain!' they heard Donkin roar, and stamp his feet with such effect that the floor opened, and down through the square of light came the cashier feet first.

'Heaven and hell!' he squealed, but subsided unhurt on hands and knees as the flaps went up with such a snap that Macbean and Carrick nudged each other at the same moment. 'Now I know who you are!' the cashier raved. 'Call yourself Stingaree! You're

Fowler dressed up, and this is one of Macbean's putrid practical jokes. I saw his jackal hurrying in to say I was coming. By cripes! it takes a surgical operation to see their sort, I grant you.'

There was a noise of subdued laughter overhead; even in the pit a dry chuckle came through Macbean's set teeth.

'If it's practical joke o' mine, Donkin, it's recoiled on my own poor pate,' said the old man. 'I've a rib stove in, too, if that's any consolation to ye. It's Stingaree, my manny!'

'You're right, it is, it must be!' cried the cashier, finding his words in a torrent. 'I was going to tell you. He's been at his game down south; stuck up our own mail again only yesterday, between this and Deniliquin, and got a fine haul of registered letters, so they say. But where the deuce are we? I never knew there was a cellar under here, let alone a trap-door that might have been made for these villains.'

'It was made for them,' replied Macbean, after a pause; and in the dead dark he went on to relate the frank and humble history of the hole, from its inception to the crooked climax of that bitter hour. A braver confession Fergus had never heard; its philosophic flow was unruffled by the more and more scornful interjections of the ungenerous cashier; and yet his younger countryman, who might have been proud of him, hardly listened to a word uttered by Macbean.

Half-a-dozen fallen from the lips of Donkin had lightened young Carrick's darkness with consuming fires of shame. 'A fine haul of registered letters' — among others his own last letter to his sister! So it was he who had done it all; and he had perjured himself to his benefactor, besides, betraying him. He sat in the dark between fire and ice, chiefly wondering how he could soonest win through the trap-door and earn a bullet in his brain.

'The spree to-night,' concluded Macbean, whose fall completely sobered him, 'was for the express purpose of expounding the trap to you, and I asked you airly to take your advice. I was no so sure about young Fowler, whether we need tell him or no. He has an awful long tongue; but I'm thinkin' there's a longer if I knew where to look for it.'

'I could tell you where,' rasped Donkin. 'But go on.'

'I was watching old Hannah putting her feenishing touches to the table, and waiting for Fergus Carrick to come back, when I thought I heard him behind me and you with him. But it was Stingaree and his mate, and the two of us were covered with revolvers like young rifles. Hannah they told to go on with what she was doing, as they were mighty hungry, and I advised her to do as she was bid. The brute with the beard has charge of her. Stingaree himself drove me into the middle of my own trap-door, made me give up my keys, and then went behind the counter and did the trick. He'd got it all down on paper, the Lord alone knows how.'

'Oh, you Scotchmen!' cried the pleasant cashier. 'Talk of your land of cakes! You take every cake in the land between you!'

It seemed he had been filling his pipe while he listened and prepared this pretty speech. Now he struck a match, and with the flame to the bowl saw Fergus for the first time. The cashier held the match on high.

'You hear all the while?' he cried. 'No wonder you lay low, Carrick; no wonder I didn't hear your voice.'

'What do you mean by that?' growled Fergus, in fierce heat and fierce satisfaction.

'Surely, Mr. Macbean, you aren't wondering who wagged the long tongue now?'

'You mean that I wagged mine? And it's a lie!' said Fergus, hoarsely; he was sitting upon his heels, poised to spring.

'I mean that if Mr. Macbean had listened to me two months ago we should none of us be in this hole now.'

'Then, my faith, you're in a worse one than

you think!' cried Fergus, and fell upon his traducer as the match went out. 'Take that, and that, and that!' he ground out through his teeth, as he sent the cashier over on his back and pounded the earth with his skull. Luckily the first was soft and the second hard, so that the man was more outraged than hurt when circumstances which they might have followed created a diversion.

In his turn the lively Fowler had marched whistling into the bank, had ceased whistling to swear down the barrel of a cocked revolver, and met a quicker fate than his comrades by impressing the bushranger as the most dangerous man of the quartette. Unfortunately for him, his fate was still further differentiated from theirs. Fowler's feet glanced off Carrick's back, and he plunged into the well head-first, rolling over like a stone as the wooden jaws above closed greedily upon the light of day.

Fergus at once struck matches, and in their light the cashier took the insensible head upon his knees and glared at his enemy as if from sanctuary of the Red Cross. But Fergus returned to Macbean's side.

'I never said a word to a living soul,' he muttered. 'It has come out some other way.'

'Of course it has,' said the old manager, with the same tell-tale inhalation through the teeth. Fergus felt worse than ever. He groped for the bald head and found it cold and dank. In an instant he was clamoring under the trap-door, leaping up and striking it with his fist.

'What do you want?'

'Whiskey. Some of us are hurt.'

'God help you if it's any hanky-panky!'

'It's none. Something to drink, and something to drink it in, or there's blood upon your head!'

Clanking steps departed and returned.

'Stand by to catch, below there!'

And Fergus stood by, expecting to see a long barrel with the bottle and glass that broke their fall on him; but Stingaree had crept away unheard, and he pressed the lever just enough to let the glass and bottle tumble through.

Time passed: it might have been an hour. The huddled heap that was Macbean breathed forth relief. The head on Donkin's knees moved from side to side with groans. Donkin himself thanked Fergus for his ration; he who served it out alone went thirsty. 'Wait till I earn some,' he said bitterly to himself. 'I could finish the lot if I started now.' But the others never dreamt that he was waiting, and he lied about it to Macbean.

Now that they sat in silence no sound

escaped them overhead. They heard Stingaree and his mate sit down to a feast which Macbean described with groaning modesty as the best that he could do.

'There's no soup,' he whispered, 'but there's a barr'l of oysters fetched up on purpose by the coach. I hope they havena missed the Chablis. They may as well do the thing complete.' In a little the champagne popped. 'Dry Monopole!' moaned the manager, near to tears. 'It came up along with the oysters. O sirs, O sirs, but this is hard on us all! Now they're at the turkey — and I chopped the stuffing with my ain twa han's!'

They were at the turkey a long time. Another cork popped; but the familiar tread of deaf Hannah was heard no more, and at length they called her.

'Mother!' roared a mouth that was full.

'Old lady!' cried the gallant Stingaree.

'She's 'ard of' earing, mate.'

'She might still hear you, Howie.'

And the chairs rasped backward over bare boards as one; at the same instant Fergus leapt to his feet in the earthly Tartarus his own hands had dug.

'I do believe she's done a bolt,' he gasped, 'and got clean away!'

Curses overhead confirmed the supposition. Clanking feet hunted the premises at a run. In a minute the curses were renewed and multiplied, yet muffled, as though there was some fresh cause for them which the prisoners need not know. Hannah had not been found. Yet some disturbing discovery had undoubtedly been made. Doors were banged and bolted. A gunshot came faint but staccato from the outer world. A real report echoed through the bank.

'A siege!' cried Fergus, striking a match to dance by. 'The old heroine has fetched the police, and these beauties are in a trap.'

'And what about us?' demanded the cashier.

'Shut up and listen!' retorted Fergus, without ceremony. Macbean was leaning forward, with bald head on one side and hollowed palm at the upper ear. Even the stunned man had recovered sufficiently to raise himself on one elbow and gaze overhead as Fergus struck match after match. The villains were having an altercation on the very trap-door.

'Now's the time to cut and run — now or never.'

'Very well, you do so. I'm going through the safe.'

'You should ha' done that first.'

'Better late than not at all.'

'You can't stop and do it without me.'

'Oh, yes, I can. I'll call for a volunteer from below. You show them your spurs and save your skin.'

'Oh, I'll stay, curse you, I'll stay!'

'And I'll have my volunteer, whether you stay or not.'

The pair had scarcely parted when the trap-door opened slowly and stayed open for the first time. The banking chamber was but dimly lit, and the light in the pit less than it had been during the brief burning of single matches. No peering face was revealed to those below, but the voice of Stingaree came rich and crisp from behind the counter.

'Your old woman has got away to the police-barracks and the place is surrounded. One of you has got to come up and help, and help fair, or go to hell with a bullet in his heart. I give you one minute to choose your man.'

But in one second the man had chosen himself. Without a word, or a glance at any of his companions, but with a face burning with extraordinary fires, Fergus Carrick sprang for the clean edge of the trap-door, caught it first with one hand and then with both, drew himself up like the gymnast he had been at his Scottish school, and found himself prone upon the floor and trap-door as the latter closed under him on the release of the lever which Stingaree understood so well. A yell of execration followed him into the upper air. And Stingaree was across the counter before his new ally had picked himself up.

'That's because this was expected of me,' said Fergus, grimly, to explain the cashier's reiterated anathemas. 'I was the writer of the registered letter that led to all this. So now I'm going the whole hog.'

And the blue eyes boiled in his brick-red face.

'You mean that? No nonsense?'

'You shall see.'

'I should shoot you like a native cat.'

'You couldn't do me a better turn.'

'Right! Swear on your knees that you won't use it against me or my mate, and I'll trust you with this revolver. You may fire as high as you please, but they must think we're three instead of two.'

Fergus took the oath in fierce earnest upon his knees, was handed the weapon belonging to the bank, and posted in his own bedroom window at the rear of the building. The front was secure enough with the shutters and bolts of the official fortress. It was to the back premises that the attack confined itself, making all use of the admirable cover afforded by the stables.

Carrick saw heads and shoulders hunched

to aim over stable-doors as he obeyed his orders and kept his oath. His high fire drew a deadlier upon himself; a stream of lead from a Winchester whistled into the room past his ear and over his ducked head. He tried firing from the floor without showing his face. The Winchester let him alone; in a sudden sickness he sprang up to see if anything hung sprawling over the stable-door, and was in time to see men in retreat to right and left, the white pugarees of the police fluttering ingloriously among them. Only one was left upon the ground, and he could sit up to nurse a knee.

Fergus sighed relief as he sought Stingaree, and found him with a comical face before the open safe.

'House full of paltry paper!' said he. 'I suppose it's the old sportsman's custom to get rid of most of his heavy metal before closing on Saturdays?'

Fergus said it was; he had himself stowed many a strong-box aboard unsuspected barges for Echuca.

'Well, now's our time to leave you,' continued Stingaree. 'If I'm not mistaken, their flight is simply for the moment, and in two or three more they'll be back to batter in the bank shutters. I wonder what they think we've done with our horses? I'll bet they've looked everywhere but in the larder next the kitchen door — not that we ever let them get so close. But my mate's in there now, mounted and waiting, and I shall have to leave you.'

'But I was coming with you,' cried Fergus, aghast.

Stingaree's eye-glass dangled on its cord.

'I'm afraid I must trouble you to step into that safe instead,' said he, smiling.

'Man, I mean it! You think I don't. I've fought on your side of my own free will. How can I live that down? It's the only side for me for the rest of time!'

The fixed eye-glass covered the brick-red face with the molten eyes.

'I believe you do mean it.'

'You shall shoot me if I don't.'

'I most certainly should. But my mate Howie has his obvious limitations. I've long wanted a drop of new blood. Barmaid's thoroughbred and strong as an elephant; we're neither of us heavyweights; by the powers, I'll trust you, and you shall ride behind!'

Now, Barmaid was the milk-white mare that was only less notorious than her lawless rider. It was noised in travellers' huts and around campfires that she would do more at her master's word than had been known of horse outside a circus. It was the one touch that Stingaree had borrowed from a more Napoleonic but incomparably coarser and crueller knight of the bush. In all other respects the *fin de siècle* desperado was unique. It was a stroke of luck, however, that there happened to be an old white mare in the bank stables, which the police had impounded with solemn care while turning every other animal adrift. And so it fell out that not a shot followed the mounted bushrangers into the night, and that long before the bank shutters were battered in the flying trio were miles away.

Fergus flew like a runaway bride, his arms about the belted waist of Stingaree. Trees loomed ahead and flew past by the clump under a wonderful wide sky of scintillating stars. The broad bush track had very soon been deserted at a tangent; through ridges and billows of salt-bush and cotton-bush they sailed with the swift confidence of a well-handled clipper before the wind. Stingaree was the leader four miles out of five, but in the fifth his mate Howie would gallop ahead, and anon they would come on him dismounted at a wire fence, with the wires strapped down and his horse tethered to one of the posts till he had led Barmaid over.

It was thus they careered across the vast

chessboard of the fenced back-blocks at dead of night. Stingaree and Fergus sat saddle and bareback without a break until near dawn their pioneer spurred forward yet again and was swallowed in a steely haze. It was cold as a sharp spring night in England. But for a mile or more Fergus had clung on with but one arm round the bushranger's waist; now the right arm came stealing back; felt something cold for the fraction of a second, and plucked prodigiously, and in another fraction an icy ring mouthed Stingaree's neck.

'Pull up,' said Fergus, hoarsely, 'or your brains go flying.'

'Little traitor!' whispered the other, with an imprecation that froze the blood.

'I am no traitor. I swore I wouldn't abuse the revolver you gave me, and it's been in my pocket all the night.'

'The other's unloaded.'

'You wouldn't sit so quiet if it were. Now, round we go, and back on our tracks full split. It's getting light, and we shall see them plain. If you vary a yard either way, or if your mate catches us, out go your brains.'

The bushranger obeyed without a word. Fergus was almost unnerved by the incredible ease of his conquest over so redoubtable a ruffian. His stolid Scottish blood stood by him; but still he made grim apology as they rode.

'I had to do it. It was through me you got to know. I had to live that down; this was the only way.'

'You have spirit. If you would still be my mate — '

'Your mate! I mean this to be the making of me as an honest man. Here's the fence. I give you two minutes to strap it down and get us over.'

Stingaree slid tamely to the ground.

'Don't you dare to get through those wires! Strap it from this side with your belt, and strap it quick!'

And the bushranger obeyed with the same sensible docility, but with his back turned, so that Fergus could not see his face; and it was light enough to see faces now; yet Barmaid refused the visible wires, as she had not refused them all that night of indigo starlight.

'Coax her, man!' cried Fergus, in the saddle now, and urging the mare with his heels. So Stingaree whispered in the mare's ear; and with that the strapped wires flew under his captor's nose, as the rider took the fence, but not the horse.

At a single syllable the milk-white mare had gone on her knees, like devout lady in holy fane; and as she rose her last rider lay senseless at her master's feet; but whether from his fall, or from a blow dealt him in the act of falling, the unhappy Fergus never knew. Indeed, knowledge for him was at an end until matches burnt under his nose awakened him to a position of the last humiliation. His throat and chin topped a fence-post, the weight of his body was on chin and throat, while wrists and muscles were lashed at full stretch to the wires on either side.

'Now I'm going to shoot you like a dog,' said Stingaree. He drew the revolver whose muzzle had pressed into his own neck so short a time before. Yet now it was broad daylight, and the sun coming up in the bound youth's eyes for the last time.

'Shoot away!' he croaked, raising the top of his head to speak at all. 'I gave you leave before we started. Shoot away!'

'At ten paces,' said Stingaree, stepping them. 'That, I think, is fair.'

'Perfectly,' replied Fergus. 'But be kind enough to make this so-called man of yours hold his foul tongue till I'm out of earshot of you all.'

Huge Howie had muttered little enough for him, but to that little Stingaree put an instantaneous stop.

'He's a dog, to be shot like a dog, but too

good a dog for you to blackguard!' cried he. 'Any message, young fellow?'

'Not through you.'

'So long, then!'

'Shoot away!'

The long barrel was poised as steadily as field-gun on its carriage. Fergus kept his blue eyes on the gleaming ring of the muzzle.

The hammer fell, the cartridge cracked, and from the lifted muzzle a tiny cloud flowed like a bubble from a pipe. The post quivered under Carrick's chin, and a splinter flew up and down before his eyes. But that was all.

'Aim longer,' said he. 'Get it over this shot.'

'I'll try.'

But the same thing happened again.

'Come nearer,' sneered Fergus.

And Stingaree strode forward with an oath.

'I was going to give you six of them. But you're a braver man than I thought. And that's the lot.'

The bound youth's livid face turned redder than the red dawn.

'Shoot me — shoot!' he shouted, like a lunatic.

'No, I shall not. I never meant to — I did mean you to sit out six — but you're the most gallant little idiot I've ever struck. Besides, you come from the old country, like myself!'

And a sigh floated into the keen morning air as he looked his last upon the lad through the celebrated monocle.

'Then I'll shoot myself when I'm free,' sobbed Fergus through his teeth.

'Oh, no, you won't,' were Stingaree's last words. 'You'll find it's not a bit worth while.'

And when the mounted police and others from Glenranald discovered the trussed youngster, not an hour later, they took the same tone. And one and all stopped and stooped to peer at the two bullet-holes in the post, and at something underneath them, before cutting poor Fergus down.

Then they propped him up to read with his own eyes the nailed legend which first helped Fergus Carrick to live down the indiscretion of his letter to Largs, and then did more for him in that Colony than letter from Queen Victoria to His Excellency of New South Wales. For it ran: —

'THIS IS THE GAMEST LITTLE COCK I HAVE EVER STRUCK. HE HAD ME CAPTIVE ONCE, COULD HAVE SHOT ME OVER AND OVER AGAIN, AND ALL BUT TOOK ME ALIVE. MORE POWER TO HIM!

'STINGAREE.'

'To the Vile Dust'

Vanheimert had been in many duststorms, but never in such a storm so far from the haunts of men. Awaking in his blanket with his mouth full of sand, he had opened his eyes to the blinding sting of a storm which already shrouded the very tree under which he lay. Other landmarks there were none; the world was swallowed in a yellow swirl that turned browner and more opaque even as Vanheimert shook himself out of his blanket and ran for the fence as for his life. He had only left it in order to camp where his tree had towered against the stars; it could not be a hundred yards away; and along the fence ran that beaten track to which the bushman turned instinctively in his panic. In a few seconds he was groping with outstretched hands to break the violence of a collision with invisible wires; in a few minutes, standing at a loss, wondering where the wires or he had got to, and whether it would not be wise to retrace his steps and try again. And while he wondered a fit of coughing drove the dust from his mouth like smoke; and even as he coughed the thickening swirl obliterated his tracks as swiftly as heavy snow.

Speckled eyeballs stood out of a sanded face as Vanheimert saw himself adrift and drowning in the dust. He was a huge young fellow, and it was a great smooth face, from which the gaping mouth cut a slice from jaw to jaw. Terror and rage, and an overpowering passion of self-pity, convulsed the coarse features in turn; then, with the grunt of a wounded beast, he rallied and plunged to his destruction, deeper and deeper into the bush, further and further from the fence.

The trees were few and mostly stunted, but Vanheimert crashed into more than one upon his headlong course. The sense was choked out of him already; he was fleeing on the wings of the storm; of direction he thought no more. He forgot that the run he had been traversing was at the best abandoned by man and beast; he forgot the 'spell' that he had promised himself at the deserted homestead where he had once worked as a lad. He might have remembered that the paddock in which he was burying himself had always been the largest in the district. It was a ten-mile block without subdividing fence or drop of water from end to end. The whole station was a howling desert, little likely to be stocked a second time by enlightened man. But this was the desert's heart, and into it sped Vanheimert, coated yellow to the eyes and lips, the dust-fiend himself in visible shape. Now he staggered in his stride, now fell headlong to cough and sob in the hollow of his arm. The unfortunate young man had the courage of his desperate strait. Many times he arose and hurled himself onward with curse or prayer; many times he fell or flung himself back to earth. But at length the storm passed over and over his spent members; sand gathered by the handful in the folds of his clothes; the end was as near as end could be.

It was just then that two riders, who fancied they had heard a voice, struck an undoubted trail before it vanished, and followed it to the great sprawling body in which the dregs of life pulsed feebly. The thing groaned as it was lifted and strapped upon a horse; it gurgled gibberish at the taste of raw spirits later in the same hour. It was high noon before Vanheimert opened a seeing eye and blinked it in the unveiled sun.

He was lying on a blanket in a treeless hollow in the midst of trees. The ground had been cleared by no human hand; it was a little basin of barren clay, burnt to a brick, and drained by the tiny water-hole that sparkled through its thatch of leaves and branches in the centre of a natural circle. Vanheimert lay

70

on the eastern circumference; it was the sun falling sheer on his upturned face that cut short his sleep of deep exhaustion. The sky was a dark and limpid blue; but every leaf within Vanheimert's vision bore its little load of sand, and the sand was clotted as though the dust-storm had ended with the usual shower. Vanheimert turned and viewed the sylvan amphitheatre; on its far side were two small tents, and a man in a folding chair reading the *Australasian*. He closed the paper on meeting Vanheimert's eyes, went to one of the tents, stood a moment looking in, and then came across the sunlit circle with his newspaper and the folded chair.

'And how do you feel now?' said he, setting up the chair beside the blanket, but still standing as he surveyed the prostrate man, with dark eyes drawn together in the shade of a great straw sombrero.

'Fine!' replied Vanheimert, huskily. 'But where am I, and who are you chaps? Rabbiters?'

As he spoke, however, he searched for the inevitable strings of rabbit skins festooned about the tents, and found them not.

'If you like,' replied the other, frowning a little at the immediate curiosity of the rescued man.

'I don't like,' said Vanheimert, staring

unabashed. 'I'm a rabbiter myself, and know too much. It ain't no game for abandoned stations, and you don't go playin' it in top-boots and spurs. Where's your skins and where's your squatter to pay for 'em? Plucky rabbiters, you two!'

And he gazed across the open toward the further tent, which had just disgorged a long body and a black beard not wholly unfamiliar to Vanheimert. The dark man was a shade darker as he followed the look and read its partial recognition; but a grim light came with quick resolve, and it was with sardonic deliberation that an eye-glass was screwed into one dark eye.

'Then what should you say that we are?'

'How do I know?' cried Vanheimert, turning pale; for he had been one of the audience at Mrs. Clarkson's concert in Gulland's store, and in consecutive moments he had recognized first Howie and now Stingaree.

'You know well enough!'

And the terrible eye-glass covered him like a pistol.

'Perhaps I can guess,' faltered Vanheimert, no small brain working in his prodigious skull.

'Guess, then!'

'There are tales about a new chum

camping by himself — that is, just with one man — '

'And what object?'

'To get away from the world, sir.'

'And where did you hear these tales?'

'All along the road, sir.'

The chastened tone, the anxious countenance, the sudden recourse to the servile monosyllable, were none of them lost on Stingaree; but he himself had once set such a tale abroad, and it might be that the present bearer still believed it. The eyeglass looked him through and through. Vanheimert bore the inspection like a man, and was soon satisfied that his recognition of the outlaw was as yet quite unsuspected. He congratulated himself on his presence of mind, and had sufficient courage to relish the excitement of a situation of which he also perceived the peril.

'I suppose you have no recollection of how you got here?' at length said Stingaree.

'Not me. I only remember the dust-storm.' And Vanheimert shuddered where he lay in the sun. 'But I'm very grateful to you, sir, for saving my life.'

'You are, are you?'

'Haven't I cause to be, sir?'

'Well, I dare say we did bring you round between us, but it was pure luck that we ever came across you. And now I should lie quiet if I were you. In a few minutes there'll be a pannikin of tea for you, and after that you'll feel a different man.'

Vanheimert lay quiet enough; there was much to occupy his mind. Instinctively he had assumed a part, and he was only less quick to embrace the necessity of a strictly consistent performance. He watched Stingaree in close conversation with Howie, who was boiling the billy on a spirit-lamp between the two tents, but he watched them with an admirable simulation of idle unconcern. They were talking about him, of course; more than once they glanced in his direction; and each time Vanheimert congratulated himself the more heartily on the ready pretence to which he was committed. Let them but dream that he knew them, and Vanheimert gave himself as short a shrift as he would have granted in their place. But they did not dream it, they were off their guard, and rather at his mercy than he at theirs. He might prove the immediate instrument of their capture — why not? The thought put Vanheimert in a glow; on the blanket where they had laid him, he dwelt on it without a qualm; and the same wide mouth watered for the tea which these villains were making, and for their blood.

It was Howie who came over with the

steaming pannikin, and watched Vanheimert as he sipped and smacked his lips, while Stingaree at his distance watched them both. The pannikin was accompanied by a tin-plate full of cold mutton and a wedge of baking-powder bread, which between them prevented the ravening man from observing how closely he was himself observed as he assuaged his pangs. There was, however, something in the nature of a muttered altercation between the bushrangers when Howie was sent back for more of everything. Vanheimert put it down to his own demands, and felt that Stingaree was his friend when it was he who brought the fresh supplies.

'Eat away,' said Stingaree, seating himself and producing pipe and tobacco. 'It's rough fare, but there's plenty of it.'

'I won't ask you for no more,' replied Vanheimert, paving the way for his escape.

'Oh, yes, you will!' said Stingaree. 'You're going to camp with us for the next few days, my friend!'

'Why am I?' cried Vanheimert, aghast at the quiet statement, which it never occurred to him to gainsay. Stingaree pared a pipeful of tobacco and rubbed it fine before troubling to reply.

'Because the way out of this takes some finding, and what's the use of escaping an unpleasant death one day if you go and die it the next? That's one reason,' said Stingaree, 'but there's another. The other reason is that, now you're here, you don't go till I choose.'

Blue wreaths of smoke went up with the words, which might have phrased either a humorous hospitality or a covert threat. The dispassionate tone told nothing. But Vanheimert felt the eye-glass on him, and his hearty appetite was at an end.

'That's real kind of you,' said he. 'I don't feel like running no more risks till I'm obliged. My nerves are shook. And if a born back-blocker may make so bold, it's a fair old treat to see a new chum camping out for the fun of it!'

'Who told you I was a new chum?' asked Stingaree, sharply. 'Ah! I remember,' he added, nodding; 'you heard of me lower down the road.'

Vanheimert grinned from ear to ear.

'I'd have known it without that,' said he. 'What real bushmen would boil their billy on a spirit-lamp when there's wood and to spare for a camp-fire on all sides of 'em?'

Now, Vanheimert clearly perceived the superiority of smokeless spirit-lamp to telltale fire for those in hiding; so he chuckled consumedly over this thrust, which was taken in such excellent part by Stingaree as to prove him a victim to the desired illusion. It was the cleverest touch that Vanheimert had yet achieved. And he had the wit neither to blunt his point by rubbing it in nor to recall attention to it by subtle protestation of his pretended persuasion. But once or twice before sundown he permitted himself to ask natural questions concerning the old country, and to indulge in those genial gibes which the Englishman in the bush learns to expect from the indigenous buffoon.

In the night Vanheimert was less easy. He had to sleep in Howie's tent, but it was some hours before he slept at all, for Howie would remain outside, and Vanheimert longed to hear him snore. At last the rabbiter fell into a doze, and when he awoke the auspicious music filled the tent. He listened on one elbow, peering till the darkness turned less dense; and there lay Howie across the opening of the tent.

Vanheimert reached for his thin elastic-sided bushman's boots, and his hands trembled as he drew them on. He could now see the form of Howie plainly enough as it lay half in the starlight and half in the darkness of the tent. He stepped over it without a mistake, and the ignoble strains droned on behind him.

The stars seemed unnaturally bright and

busy as Vanheimert stole into their tremulous light. At first he could distinguish nothing earthly; then the tents came sharply into focus, and after them the ring of impenetrable trees. The trees whispered a chorus, myriads strong, in a chromatic scale that sang but faintly of the open country. There were palpable miles of wilderness, and none other lodge but this, yet the psychological necessity for escape was stronger in Vanheimert than the bodily reluctance to leave the insecure security of the bushrangers' encampment. He was their prisoner, whatever they might say, and the sense of captivity was intolerable; besides, let them but surprise his knowledge of their secret, and they would shoot him like a dog. On the other hand, beyond the forest and along the beaten track lay fame and a fortune in direct reward.

Before departure Vanheimert wished to peep into the other tent, but its open end was completely covered in for the night, and prudence forbade him to meddle with his hands. He had an even keener desire to steal one or other of the horses which he had seen before nightfall tethered in the scrub; but here again he lacked enterprise, fancied the saddles must be in Stingaree's tent, and shrank from committing himself to an action which nothing, in the event of disaster, could explain away. On foot he need not put himself in the wrong, even with villains ready to suspect that he suspected them.

And on foot he went, indeed on tiptoe till the edge of the trees was reached without adventure, and he turned to look his last upon the two tents shimmering in the starlight. As he turned again, satisfied that the one was still shut and that Howie still lay across the opening of the other, a firm hand took Vanheimert by either shoulder; otherwise he had leapt into the air; for it was Stingaree, who had stepped from behind a bush as from another planet, so suddenly that Vanheimert nearly gasped his dreadful name.

'I couldn't sleep! I couldn't sleep!' he cried out instead, shrinking as from a lifted hand, though he was merely being shaken playfully to and fro.

'No more could I,' said Stingaree.

'So I was going for a stroll. That was all, I swear, Mr. — Mr. — I don't know your name!'

'Quite sure?' said Stingaree.

'My oath! How should I?'

'You might have heard it down the road.'

'Not me!'

'Yet you heard of me, you know.'

'Not by name — my oath!'

Stingaree peered into the great face in

which the teeth were chattering and from which all trace of color had flown.

'I shouldn't eat you for knowing who I am,' said he. 'Honesty is still a wise policy in certain circumstances; but you know best.'

'I know nothing about you, and care less,' retorted Vanheimert, sullenly, though the perspiration was welling out of him. 'I come for a stroll because I couldn't sleep, and I can't see what all this barney's about.'

Stingaree dropped his hands.

'Do you want to sleep?'

'My blessed oath!'

'Then come to my tent, and I'll give you a nobbler that may make you.'

The nobbler was poured out of a gallon jar, under Vanheimert's nose, by the light of a candle which he held himself. Yet he smelt it furtively before trying it with his lips, and denied himself a gulp till he was reassured. But soon the empty pannikin was held out for more. And it was the starless hour before dawn when Vanheimert tripped over Howie's legs and took a contented header into the corner from which he had made his stealthy escape.

The tent was tropical when he awoke, but Stingaree was still at his breakfast outside in the shade. He pointed to a bucket and a piece of soap behind the tent, and Vanheimert engaged in obedient ablutions before sitting down to his pannikin, his slice of damper, and his portion of a tin of sardines.

'Sorry there's no meat for you,' said Stingaree. 'My mate's gone for fresh supplies. By the way, did you miss your boots?'

The rabbiter looked at a pair of dilapidated worsted socks and at one protruding toe; he was not sure whether he had gone to bed for the second time in these or in his boots. Certainly he had missed the latter on his second awakening, but had not deemed it expedient to make inquiries. And now he merely observed that he wondered where he could have left them.

'On your feet,' said Stingaree. 'My mate has made so bold as to borrow them for the day.'

'He's welcome to them, I'm sure,' said Vanheimert with a sickly smile.

'I was sure you would say so,' rejoined Stingaree. 'His own are reduced to uppers and half a heel apiece, but he hopes to get them soled in Ivanhoe while he waits.'

'So he's gone to Ivanhoe, has he?'

'He's been gone three hours.'

'Surely it's a long trip?'

'Yes; we shall have to make the most of each other till sundown,' said Stingaree, gazing through his glass upon Vanheimert's perplexity. 'If I were you I should take my revenge by shaking anything of his that I could find for the day.'

And with a cavalier nod, to clinch the last word on the subject, the bushranger gave himself over to his camp-chair, his pipe, and his inexhaustible *Australasian*. As for Vanheimert, he eventually returned to the tent in which he had spent the night; and there he remained a good many minutes, though it was now the forenoon, and the heat under canvas past endurance. But when at length he emerged, as from a bath, Stingaree, seated behind his *Australasian* in the lee of the other tent, took so little notice of him that Vanheimert crept back to have one more look at the thing which he had found in the old valise which served Howie for a pillow. And the thing was a very workmanlike revolver, with a heavy cartridge in each of its six chambers.

Vanheimert handled it with trembling fingers, and packed it afresh in the pocket where it least affected his personal contour, its angles softened by a big bandanna handkerchief, only to take it out yet again with a resolution that opened a fresh sluice in every pore. The blanket that had been lent to him, and Howie's blanket, both lay at his feet; he threw one over either arm, and with the revolver thus effectually concealed, but grasped for action with finger on trigger, sallied forth at last.

Stingaree was still seated in the narrowing shade of his own tent. Vanheimert was within five paces of him before he looked up so very quickly, with such a rapid adjustment of the terrible eye-glass, that Vanheimert stood stock-still, and the butt of his hidden weapon turned colder than ever in his melting hand.

'Why, what have you got there?' cried Stingaree. 'And what's the matter with you, man?' he added, as Vanheimert stood shaking in his socks.

'Only his blankets, to camp on,' the fellow answered, hoarsely. 'You advised me to help myself, you know.'

'Quite right; so I did; but you're as white as the tent — you tremble like a leaf. What's wrong?'

'My head,' replied Vanheimert, in a whine. 'It's going round and round, either from what I had in the night, or lying too long in the hot tent, or one on top of the other. I thought I'd camp for a bit in the shade.'

'I should,' said Stingaree, and buried himself in his paper with undisguised contempt.

Vanheimert came a step nearer. Stingaree did not look up again. The revolver was levelled under one trailing blanket. But the trigger was never pulled. Vanheimert feared to miss even at arm's length, so palsied was his hand, so dim his eye; and when he would have played the man and called desperately on the other to surrender, the very tongue clove in his head.

He slunk over to the shady margin of surrounding scrub and lay aloof all the morning, now fingering the weapon in his pocket, now watching the man who never once looked his way. He was a bushranger and an outlaw; he deserved to die or to be taken; and Vanheimert's only regret was that he had neither taken nor shot him at their last interview. The bloodless alternative was to be borne in mind, yet in his heart he well knew that the bullet was his one chance with Stingaree. And even with the bullet he was horribly uncertain and afraid. But of hesitation on any higher ground, of remorse or of reluctance, or the desire to give fair play, he had none at all. The man whom he had stupidly spared so far was a notorious criminal with a high price upon his head. It weighed not a grain with Vanheimert that the criminal happened to have saved his life.

'Come and eat,' shouted Stingaree at last; and Vanheimert trailed the blankets over his left arm, his right thrust idly into his pocket, which bulged with a red bandanna hand-kerchief. 'Sorry it's sardines again,' the bushranger went on, 'but we shall make up with a square feed to-night if my mate gets back by dark; if he doesn't, we may have to tighten our belts till morning. Fortunately, there's plenty to drink. Have some whiskey in your tea?'

Vanheimert nodded, and with an eye on the bushranger, who was once more stooping over his beloved *Australasian*, helped himself enormously from the gallon jar.

'And now for a siesta,' yawned Stingaree, rising and stretching himself after the meal.

'Hear, hear!' croaked Vanheimert, his great face flushed, his bloodshot eyes on fire.

'I shall camp on the shady side of my tent.'

'And I'll do ditto at the other.'

'So long, then.'

'So long.'

'Sweet repose to you!'

'Same to you,' rasped Vanheimert, and went off cursing and chuckling in his heart by turns.

It was a sweltering afternoon of little air, and that little as hot and dry in the nostrils as the atmosphere of a laundry on ironing day. Beyond and above the trees a fiery blast blew from the north; but it was seldom a wandering puff stooped to flutter the edges of the tents in the little hollow among the trees. And into this empty basin poured a vertical sun, as if through some giant lens which had burnt a hole in the heart of the scrub. Lulled by the faint perpetual murmur of leaf and branch, without a sound from bird or beast to break its soothing monotone, the two men lay down within a few yards, though out of sight, of each other. And for a time all was very still.

Then Vanheimert rose slowly, without a sound, and came on tiptoe to the other tent, his right hand in the pocket where the bandanna handkerchief had been but was no longer. He came close up to the sunny side of the tent and listened vainly for a sound. But Stingaree lay like a log in the shade on the far side, his face to the canvas and his straw sombrero tilted over it. And so Vanheimert found him, breathing with the placid regularity of a sleeping child.

Vanheimert looked about him; only the ring of impenetrable trees and the deep blue eye of Heaven would see what really happened. But as to what exactly was to happen Vanheimert himself was not clear as he drew the revolver ready cocked; even he shrank from shooting a sleeping man; what he desired and yet feared was a sudden start, a semblance of resistance, a swift, justifiable shot. And as his mind's eye measured the dead man at his feet, the live man turned slowly over on his back.

It was too much for Vanheimert's nerves. The revolver went off in his hands. But it was only a cap that snapped, and another, and another, as he stepped back firing desperately. Stingaree sat upright, looking his treacherous enemy in the eye, through the glass in which, it seemed, he slept. And when the sixth cap snapped as harmlessly as the other five, Vanheimert caught the revolver by its barrel to throw or to strike. But the raised arm was seized from behind by Howie, who had crept from the scrub at the snapping of the first cap; at the same moment Stingaree sprang upon him; and in less than a minute Vanheimert lay powerless, grinding his teeth, foaming and bleeding at the mouth, and filling the air with nameless imprecations.

The bushrangers let him curse; not a word did they bandy with him or with each other. Their action was silent, swift, concerted, prearranged. They lashed their prisoner's wrists together, lashed his elbows to his ribs, hobbled his ankles, and tethered him to a tree by the longest and the stoutest of their many ropes. The tree was the one under which Vanheimert had found himself the day before; in the afternoon it was exposed to the full fury of the sun; and in the sun they left him, quieter already, but not so quiet as they. It was near sundown when they returned to look upon a broken man, crouching in his toils like a beaten beast, with undying malice in his swollen eyes. Stingaree sat at his prisoner's feet, offered him tobacco without a sneer, and lit up his own when the offer was declined with a curse.

'When we came upon you yesterday morning in the storm, one of us was for leaving you to die in your tracks,' began Stingaree. He was immediately interrupted by his mate.

'That was me!' cried Howie, with a savage satisfaction.

'It doesn't matter which of us it was,' continued Stingaree; 'the other talked him over; we put you on one of our horses, and we brought you more dead than alive to the place which no other man has seen since we took a fancy to it. We saved your miserable life, I won't say at the risk of our own, but at risk enough even if you had not recognized us. We were going to see you through, whether you knew us or not; before this we should have set you on the road from which you had strayed. I thought you must know us by sight, but when you denied it I saw no reason to disbelieve you. It only dawned on me by degrees that you were lying, though

Howie here was sure of it.

'I still couldn't make out your game; if it was funk I could have understood it; so I tried to get you to own up in the night. I let you see that we didn't mind whether you knew us or not, and yet you persisted in your lie. So then I smelt something deeper. But we had gone out of our way to save your life. It never struck me that you might go out of your way to take ours!'

Stingaree paused, smoking his pipe.

'But it did me!' cried Howie.

'I never meant taking your lives,' muttered Vanheimert. 'I meant taking you — as you deserved.'

'We scarcely deserved it of you; but that is a matter of opinion. As for taking us alive, no doubt you would have preferred to do so if it had seemed equally safe and easy; you had not the pluck to run a single risk. You were given every chance. I sent Howie into the scrub, took the powder out of six cartridges, and put what anybody would have taken for a loaded revolver all but into your hands. I sat at your mercy, quite looking forward to the sensation of being stuck up for a change. If you had stuck me up like a man,' said Stingaree, reflectively examining his pipe, 'you might have lived to tell the tale.'

There was an interval of the faint,

persistent rustling of branch and leaf, varied by the screech of a distant cockatoo and the nearer cry of a crow, as the dusk deepened into night as expeditiously as on the stage. Vanheimert was not awed by the quiet voice to which he had been listening. It lacked the note of violence which he understood; it even lulled him into a belief that he would still live to tell the tale. But in the dying light he looked up, and in the fierce unrelenting face, made the more sinister by its foppish furniture, he read his doom.

'You tried to shoot me in my sleep,' said Stingaree, speaking slowly, with intense articulation. 'That's your gratitude! You will live just long enough to wish that you had shot yourself instead!'

Stingaree rose.

'You may as well shoot me now!' cried Vanheimert, with a husky effort.

'Shoot you? I'm not going to *shoot* you at all; shooting's too good for scum like you. But you are to die — make no mistake about that. And soon; but not to-night. That would not be fair on you, for reasons which I leave to your imagination. You will lie where you are to-night; and you will be watched and fed like your superiors in the condemned cell. The only difference is that I can't tell you when it will be. It might be to-morrow — I don't think it will — but you may number your days on the fingers of both hands.'

So saying, Stingaree turned on his heel, and was lost to sight in the shades of evening before he reached his tent. But Howie remained on duty with the condemned man.

As such Vanheimert was treated from the first hour of his captivity. Not a rough word was said to him; and his own unbridled outbursts were received with as much indifference as the abject prayers and supplications which were their regular reaction. The ebbing life was ordered on that principle of high humanity which might be the last refinement of calculated cruelty. The prisoner was so tethered to such a tree that it was no longer necessary for him to spend a moment in the red eye of the sun. He could follow a sufficient shade from dawn to dusk. His boots were restored to him; a blanket was permitted him day and night; but night and day he was sedulously watched, and neither knife nor fork was provided with his meals. His fare was relatively not inferior to that of the legally condemned, whose notorious privileges and restrictions served the bushrangers for a model.

And Vanheimert clung to the hope of a reprieve with all the sanguine tenacity of his ill-starred class, though it did seem with more encouragement on the whole. For the days went on, and each of many mornings brought its own respite till the next. The welcome announcement was invariably made by Howie after a colloquy with his chief, which Vanheimert watched with breathless interest for a day or two, but thereafter with increasing coolness. They were trying to frighten him; they did not mean it, any more than Stingaree had meant to shoot the new chum who had the temerity to put a pistol to his head after the affair of the Glenranald bank. The case of lucky Fergus, justly celebrated throughout the colony, was a great comfort to Vanheimert's mind; he could see but little difference between the two; but if his treachery was the greater, so also was the ordeal to which he was being subjected. For in the light of a mere ordeal he soon regarded what he was invited to consider as his last days on earth, and in the conviction that they were not, began suddenly to bear them like a man. This change of front produced its fellow in Stingaree, who apologized to Vanheimert for the delay, which he vowed he could not help.

Vanheimert was a little shaken by his manner, though he smiled behind the bushranger's back. And he could scarcely believe his ears when, the very next morning,

Howie told him that his hour was come.

'Rot!' said Vanheimert, with a confident expletive.

'Oh, all right,' said Howie. 'But if you don't believe me, I'm sorrier for you than I was.'

He slouched away, but Vanheimert had no stomach for the tea and damper which had been left behind. It was unusual for him to be suffered to take a meal unwatched; something unusual was in the air. Stingaree emerged from the scrub leading the two horses. Vanheimert began to figure the fate that might be in store for him. And the horses, saddled and bridled before his eyes, were led over to where he sat.

'Are you going to shoot me before you go,' he cried, 'or are you going to leave me to die alone?'

'Neither, here,' said Stingaree. 'We're too fond of the camp.'

It was his first brutal speech, but the brutality was too subtle for Vanheimert. He was beginning to feel that something dreadful might happen to him after all. The pinions were removed from his arms and legs, the long rope detached from the tree and made fast to one of Stingaree's stirrups instead. And by it Vanheimert was led a good mile through the scrub, with Howie at his heels.

A red sun had risen on the camp, but in the

scrub it ceased to shine, and the first open space was as sunless as the dense bush. Spires of sand kept whirling from earth to sky, joining other spinning spires, forming a monster balloon of yellow sand, a balloon that swelled until it burst, obscuring first the firmament and then the earth. But the mind of Vanheimert was so busy with the fate he feared that he did not realize he was in another dust-storm until Stingaree, at the end of the rope, was swallowed like a tug in a fog. And even then Vanheimert's peculiar terror of a dust-storm did not link itself to the fear of sudden death which had at last been put into him. But the moment of mental enlightenment was at hand.

The rope trailed on the ground as Stingaree loomed large and yellow through the storm. He had dropped his end. Vanheimert glanced over his shoulder, and Howie loomed large and yellow behind him.

'You will now perceive the reason for so many days' delay,' said Stingaree. 'I have been waiting for such a dust-storm as the one from which we saved you, to be rewarded as you endeavored to reward me. You might, perhaps, have preferred me to make shorter work of you, but on consideration you will see that this is not only just but generous. The chances are perhaps against you, and somewhat in favor of a more unpleasant death; but it is quite possible that the storm may pass before it finishes you, and that you may then hit the fence before you die of thirst, and at the worst we leave you no worse off than we found you. And that, I hold, is more than you had any right to expect. So long!'

The thickening storm had swallowed man and horse once more. Vanheimert looked round. The second man and the second horse had also vanished. And his own tracks were being obliterated as fast as footmarks in blinding snow . . .

A Bushranger at Bay

The Hon. Guy Kentish was trotting the globe — an exercise foreign to his habit — when he went on to Australia for a reason racy of his blood. He wished to witness a certain game of cricket between the full strength of Australia and an English team which included one or two young men of his acquaintance. It was no part of his original scheme to see anything of the country; one of the Australian cricketers put that idea into his head; and it was under inward protest that Mr. Kentish found himself smoking his chronic cigar on the Glenranald and Clear Corner coach one scorching morning in the month of February. He thought he had never seen such a howling desert in his life; and it is to be feared that in his heart he applied the same epithet to his two fellow-passengers. The one outside was chatting horribly with the driver; the other had tried to chaff the Hon. Guy, and had repaired in some disorder to the company of the mail-bags inside. Kentish wondered whether these were the types he might expect to encounter upon the station to which he had reluctantly accepted an officious introduction. He wished himself out of the absurd little two-horse coach, out of an expedition whose absurdity was on a larger scale, and back again on the shady side of the two or three streets where he lived his normal life. The fare at wayside inns made the thought of his club a positive pain; and these pangs were at their sharpest when Stingaree cantered out of the scrub on his lily mare, a blessed bolt from the blue.

Mr. Kentish watched the little operation of 'sticking up' without a word, but with revived interest in life. He noted the pusillanimous pallor of the driver and his friend, and felt personally indebted to the desperado who had put a stop to their unpleasant conversation. The inside passenger made a yet more obsequious surrender. Not that the trio were set any better example by their noble ally, who began by smiling at the whole affair, and was content to the last in taking an observant interest in the bushranger's methods. These were simple and in a sense humane; there was no personal robbery at all. The mail-bags were sufficient for Stingaree, who on this occasion worked alone, but led a pack-horse, to which the driver and the inside passenger were compelled to strap the long canvas bags, under his eye-glass and his long revolver. Few words were spoken from first to last; the Hon.

Guy never put in his at all; but he watched the outlaw like a lynx, without betraying an undue attention, and when all was over he gave a sigh.

'So that's Stingaree!' he said, more to himself than to his comrades in humiliation; but the bushranger had cantered back into the scrub, and his name opened the flood-gates of a profanity which made Kentish wince, for all his knowledge of the world.

'Do you never swear at him till he has gone?' he asked when he had a chance. The driver leant across the legs of his friend.

'Not unless we want a bullet through our skulls,' he answered in boorish derision; and the man between them laughed harshly.

'I thought he had never been known to shoot?'

'That's just it, mister. We don't want him to begin on us.'

'Why didn't *you* give him a bit of *your* mind?' the man in the middle inquired of Kentish. 'I never heard you open your gills!'

'And we expected to see some pluck from the old country,' added the driver, wreaking vengeance with his lash.

Mr. Kentish produced his cigar-case with an insensitive smile, and, after a moment's deliberation, handed it for the first time to his uncouth companions. 'Do you want those mail-bags back?' he asked, quite casually, when the three cigars were in blast.

'Want them? Of course I want them; but want must be my boss,' said the driver, gloomily.

'I'm not so sure,' said Kentish. 'When does the next coach pass this way?'

'Midnight, and I drive it. I turn back when I get to Clear Corner, you see.'

'Then look out for me about this spot. I'm going to ask you to put me down.'

'Put you down?'

'If you don't mind pulling up. I'm not going on at present; but I'll go back with you to Glenranald instead, if you'll keep a lookout for me to-night.'

Instinctively the driver put his foot upon the brake, for the request had been made with that quiet authority which this silent passenger had suddenly assumed; and yet it seemed to them such a mad demand that his companions looked at Kentish as they had not looked before. His face bore a close inspection; it was one of those which burn red, and in the redness twinkled hazel eyes that toned agreeably with a fair beard and fairer mustache. The former he had grown upon his travels; but the trail of the West-end tailor, whose shooting-jacket is as distinctive as his frock-coat, was upon Guy Kentish from head to heel. As they watched him he took an open envelope from his pocket, scribbled a few words on a card, put that in, and stuck down the flap.

'Here,' said he, 'is my letter of introduction to the good people at the Mazeppa Station higher up. If I don't turn up to-night, see that they get it, even if it costs you a bit of this?'

And, putting a sovereign in a startled palm, he jumped to the ground.

'But what are you going to do, sir?' cried the driver, in alarm.

'Recover your mail-bags if I can.'

'What? After you've just been stuck up — '

'Exactly. I hope to stick up Stingaree!'

'Then you were armed all the time?'

Mr. Kentish smiled as he shook his head.

'That's my affair, I imagine; but even so I am not fool enough to tackle such a fellow with his own weapons. You leave it to me, and don't be anxious. But I must be off if I'm to stalk him before he goes through the letters. No, I know what I'm doing, and I shall do better alone. Till to-night, then!'

And he was in the scrub ere they decided to take him at his madcap word, and let his blood be on the chuckle-head of the new-chummiest new chum that ever came out after the rain! Was it pluck or all pretence?

It was rather plucky even to pretend in such proximity to the terrible Stingaree; on the whole, the coaching trio were disposed to concede a certain amount of unequivocal courage; and the driver, with Kentish's sovereign in his pocket, went so far as to declare that duty alone nailed him to the box.

Meantime the Hon. Guy had skirted the road until he came to double horse-tracks striking back into the bush; these he followed with the wary stealth of one who had spent his autumns, at least, in the right place. They led him through belts of scrub in which he trod like a cat, without disturbing an avoidable branch, and over treeless spaces that he crossed at a run, bent double; but always, as he followed the trail, his shadow fell at one consistent angle, showing how the bushranger rode through his natural element as the crow might have flown overhead.

At last Kentish found himself in a sandy gully bristling with pines, through which the sunlight dripped like melted gold; and in the fine warp and woof of high light and sharp shadow the bushranger's horses stood lashing at the flies with their long tails. The bushranger himself was nowhere to be seen. But at last Kentish descried a white-and-brown litter on either side of the thickest trunk in sight, from whose further side floated intermittent puffs of thin blue smoke. Kentish looked and looked again before advancing. But the tall pine threw such a shadow as should easily swallow his own. And in another minute he was peeping round the hole.

The litter on either side was, of course, the shower of miscellaneous postal matter from the mail-bags; and in its midst sat Stingaree against the tree, enjoying his pipe and a copy of *Punch*, of which the wrapper lay upon his knees. Kentish peered for torn envelopes and gaping packets; there were no more. The bushranger had evidently started with *Punch*, and was still curiously absorbed in its contents. The notorious eye-glass dangled against that kindred vanity, the spotless white jacket which he affected in summer-time; the brown, attentive face, even as Kentish saw it in less than profile, was thus purged of the sinister aspect which such an appendage can impart to the most innocent; and a somewhat passive amusement was its unmistakable note. Nevertheless, the long revolver which had once more done its nefarious work still lay ready to his hand; indeed, the Hon. Guy could have stooped and whipped it up, had he been so minded.

He was absorbed, however, in the absorption of Stingaree; and as he peered audaciously over the other's shoulder he put himself in the outlaw's place. An old friend would have lurked in every cut, a friend whom it might well be a painful pleasure to meet again. There were the oval face and the short upper lip of one imperishable type; on the next page one of *Punch's* Fancy Portraits, with lines underneath which set Stingaree incongruously humming a stave from *H.M.S. Pinafore*. Mr. Kentish smiled without surprise. The common folk in the omnibus opposite were the common folk of an inveterate master; there was matter for a homesick sigh in his hint of streaming streets — and Kentish thought he heard one as he held his breath. The page after that detained the reader some minutes. The illustrations proclaimed it an article on the new Savoy opera, and Stingaree confirmed the impression by humming more *Pinafore* when he came to the end. Kentish left him at it, and, creeping away as silently as he had come, described a circle and came noisily on the bushranger from the front. The result was that Stingaree was not startled into firing, but stopped the intruder at due distance with his revolver levelled across the open copy of *Punch*.

'I heard you singing *Pinafore*,' cried

Kentish, cheerily. 'And I find you reading *Punch*!'

'How dare you find me?' demanded the bushranger, black with passion.

'I thought you wouldn't mind. I am perfectly innocuous — look!'

And, divesting himself of his shooting-coat, he tossed it across for the other's inspection; he wore neither waistcoat nor hip-pocket, and his innocence of arms was manifest when he had turned round slowly where he stood.

'Now may I not come a little nearer?' asked the Hon. Guy.

'No; keep your distance, and tell me why you have come so far. The truth, mind, or you'll be shot!'

'Very well,' said Kentish. 'They were dreadful people on the coach — '

'Are they waiting for you?' thundered Stingaree.

'No; they've gone on; and they think me mad.'

'So you are.'

'We shall see; meanwhile I prefer your company to theirs, and mean to enjoy it up to the moment of my murder.'

For an instant Stingaree seemed on the brink of a smile; then his dark face hardened, and he tapped the long barrel in rest between his knees.

'You may call it murder if you like,' said he. 'That will not prevent me from shooting you dead unless you speak the truth. You have come for something; what is it?'

'I've told you already. I was bored and disgusted. That is the truth.'

'But not the whole truth,' cried Stingaree. 'You had some other reason.'

Kentish looked down without speaking. He heard the revolver cocked.

'Come, let us have it, or I'll shoot you like the spy I believe you are!'

'You may shoot me for telling you,' said Kentish, with a quiet laugh and shrug.

'No, I shall not, unless it turns out that you're ground-bait for the police.'

'That I am not,' said Kentish, growing serious in his turn. 'But, since you insist, I have come to persuade you to give up every one of these letters which you have no earthly right to touch.'

Their eyes met. Stingaree's were the wider open, and in an instant the less stern. He dropped his revolver, with a laugh, into its old place at his side.

'Mad or sane,' said he, 'I shall be under the unpleasant necessity of leaving you rather securely tied to one of these trees.'

'I don't believe you will,' returned Kentish, without losing a shade of his rich coloring.

'But in any case I suppose we may have a chat first? I give you my word that you are safe from further intrusion to the level best of my knowledge and belief. May I sit down instead of standing?'

'You may.'

'We are a good many yards apart.'

'You may reduce them by half. There.'

'I thank you,' said Kentish, seating himself tailorwise within arm's length of Stingaree's spurs. 'Now, if you will feel in the breast-pocket of my coat you will find a case of very fair cigars — J. S. Murias — not too strong. I shall be honored if you will help yourself and throw me one.'

Stingaree took the one, and handed the case with no ungraceful acknowledgment to its owner; but before Mr. Kentish could return the courtesy by proffering his cigar-cutter, the bushranger had produced his razor from a pocket of the white jacket, and sliced off the end with that.

'So you shave every day in the wilds,' remarked the other, handing his match-box instead. 'And I gave it up on my voyage.'

'I alter myself from time to time,' said Stingaree, as he struck a light.

'It must be a wonderful life!'

But Stingaree lit up without a word, and Kentish had the wit to do the same. They smoked in silence for some minutes. A gray ash had grown on each cigar before Kentish demanded an opinion of the brand.

'To tell you the truth,' said Stingaree, 'I have smoked strong trash so many years that I can scarcely taste it.'

And he peered rather pathetically through his glass.

'Didn't the same apply to *Punch*?'

'No; I have always read the papers when I could,' said Stingaree, and suddenly he was smiling. 'That's one reason why I make a specialty of sticking up the mail,' he explained.

Mr. Kentish was not to be drawn into a second deliverance on the bushranging career. 'Is it a good number?' he asked, nodding toward the copy of *Punch*. The bushranger picked it up.

'Good enough for me.'

'What date?'

'Ninth of December.'

'Nearly three months ago. I was in London then,' remarked Kentish, in a reflective tone.

'Really?' cried Stingaree, under his breath. His voice was as soft as the other's, but there was suppressed interest in his manner. His dark eyes were only less alight than the red cigar he took from his teeth as he spoke. And he held it like a connoisseur, between finger and thumb, for all his ruined palate.

'I was,' repeated Kentish. 'I didn't sail till the middle of the month.'

'To think you were in town till nearly Christmas!' and Stingaree gazed enviously. 'It must be hard to realize,' he added in some haste.

'Other things,' replied Kentish, 'are harder.'

'I gather from the *Punch* cartoon that the new Law Courts are in use at last?'

'I was at the opening.'

'Then you may have seen this opera that I have been reading about?'

Kentish asked what it was, although he knew.

'*Iolanthe.*'

'Rather! I was there the first night.'

'The deuce you were!' cried Stingaree; and for the next quarter of an hour this armed scoundrel, the terror of a district as large as England and Wales, talked of nothing else to the man whom he was about to bind to a tree. Was the new opera equal to its predecessors? Which were the best numbers? Did *Punch* do it justice, or was there some jealousy in that rival hot-bed of wit and wisdom?

Unfortunately, Guy Kentish had no ear for music, but he made a clear report of the plot, could repeat some of the Lord Chancellor's quips, and was in decided disagreement with the captious banter from which he was given more than one extract. And in default of one of the new airs Stingaree rounded off the subject by dropping once more into —

'For he might have been a Rooshian,
A French, or Turk,
    or Prooshian, Or, perhaps, I-tal-i-an!
    Or, perhaps, I-tal-i-an!
But in spite of all temptations
To belong to other nations
    He remains an Englishman!'

'I understand that might be said of both of us,' remarked Kentish, looking the outlaw boldly in the eyes. 'But from all accounts I should have thought you were out here before the days of Gilbert and Sullivan.'

'So I was,' replied Stingaree, without frown or hesitation. 'But you may also have heard that I am fond of music — any I can get. My only opportunities, as a rule,' the bushranger continued, smiling mischievously at his cigar, 'occur on the stations I have occasion to visit from time to time. On one a good lady played and sang *Pinafore* and *The Pirates of Penzance* to me from dewy eve to dawn. I'm bound to say I sang some of it at sight myself; and I flatter myself it helped to pass an embarrassing night rather pleasantly for all concerned. We had all hands on the place for our audience, and when I left I was formally presented with both scores; for I had simply called for horses, and horses were all I took. Only the other day I had the luck to confiscate a musical-box which plays selections from *The Pirates*. I ought to have had it with me in my swag.'

So affable and even charming was the quiet voice, so evident the appreciation of the last inch of the cigar which had thawed a frozen palate, and so conceivable a further softening, that Guy Kentish made bolder than before. He knew what he meant to do; he knew how he meant to do it. And yet it seemed just possible there might be a gentler way.

'You don't always take things, I believe?' he hazarded.

'You mean after sticking up?'

'Yes.'

'Generally, I fear; it's the whole meaning of the act,' confessed Stingaree, still the dandy in tone and phrase. 'But there have been exceptions.'

'Exactly!' quoth Kentish. 'And there's going to be another this afternoon!'

Stingaree hurled the stump of his cigar into the scrub, and without a word the villain was born again, with his hard eyes, his harder mouth, his sinister scowl, his crag of a chin.

'So you come back to that,' he cried, harshly. 'I thought you had more sense; you will make me tie you up before your time.'

'You may do exactly what you like,' retorted Kentish, a galling scorn in his unaltered voice. 'Only, before you do it, you may as well know who I am.'

'My good sir, do you suppose I care who you are?' asked Stingaree, with an angry laugh: and his anger is the rarest thing in all his annals.

'I am quite sure you don't,' responded Kentish. 'But you may as well know my name, even though you never heard it before.' And he gave it with a touch of triumph, not for one moment to be confounded with a natural pride.

The bushranger stared him steadily in the eyes; his hand had dropped once more upon the butt of his revolver. 'No; I never did hear it before,' he said.

'I'm not surprised,' replied the other. 'I was a new member when you were turned out of the club.' Stingaree's hand closed: his eyes were terrible. 'And yet,' continued Kentish, 'the moment I saw you at close quarters in the road I recognized you as — '

'Stingaree!' cried the bushranger, on a rich

and vibrant note. 'Let the other name pass your lips — even here — and it's the last word that ever will!'

'Very well,' said Mr. Kentish, with his unaffected shrug. 'But, you see, I know all about you.'

'You're the only man who does, in all Australia!' exclaimed the outlaw, hoarsely.

'At present! I sha'n't be the only man long.'

'You will,' said Stingaree through teeth and mustache; and he leaned over, revolver in hand. 'You'll be the only man ever, because, instead of tying you up, I'm going to shoot you.'

Kentish threw up his head in sharp contempt.

'What!' said he. 'Sitting?'

Stingaree sprang to his feet in a fury. 'No; I have a brace!' he cried, catching the pack-horse. 'You shall have the other, if it makes you happy; but you'll be a dead man all the same. I can handle these things, and I shall shoot to kill!'

'Then it's all up with you,' said Kentish, rising slowly in his turn.

'All up with me? What the devil do you mean?'

'Unless I am at a certain place by a certain time, with or without these letters that are not yours, another letter will be opened.'

Stingaree's stare gradually changed into a smile.

'A little vague,' said he, 'don't you think?'

'It shall be as plain as you please. The letter I mean was scribbled on the coach before I got down. It will only be opened if I don't return. It contains the name you can't bear to hear!'

There was a pause. The afternoon sun was sinking with southern precipitancy, and Kentish had got his back to it by cool intent. He studied the play of suppressed mortification and strenuous philosophy in the swarthy face warmed by the reddening light; and admired the arduous triumph of judgment over instinct, even as a certain admiration dawned through the monocle which insensibly focussed his attention.

'And suppose,' said Stingaree — 'suppose you return empty as you came?' A contemptuous kick sent a pack of letters spinning.

'I should feel under no obligation to keep your secret.'

'And you think I would trust you to keep it otherwise?'

'If I gave you my word,' said Kentish, 'I know you would.'

Stingaree made no immediate answer; but he gazed in the sun-flayed face without suspicion.

'You wouldn't give me your word,' he said at last.

'Oh, yes, I would.'

'That you would die without letting that name pass your lips?'

'Unless I die delirious — with all my heart. I have as much respect for it as you.'

'As much!' echoed the bushranger, in a strange blend of bitterness and obligation. 'But how could you explain the bags? How could you have taken them from me?'

Kentish shrugged once more.

'You left them — I found them. Or you were sleeping, but I was unarmed.'

'You would lie like that — to save my name?'

'And a man whom I remember perfectly . . .'

Stingaree heard no more; he was down on his knees, collecting the letters into heaps and shovelling them into the bags. Even the copy of *Punch* and the loose wrapper went in with the rest.

'You can't carry them,' said he, when none remained outside. 'I'll take them for you and dump them on the track.'

'I have to pass the time till midnight. I can manage them in two journeys.'

But Stingaree insisted, and presently stood ready to mount his mare.

'You give me your word, Kentish?'

'My word of honor.'

'It is something to have one to give! I shall not come back this way; we shall have the Clear Corner police on our tracks by moonlight, and the more they have to choose from the better. So I must go. You have given me your word; you wouldn't care to give me — '

But his hand went out a little as he spoke, and Kentish's met it seven-eights of the way.

'Give this up, man! It's a poor game, when all's said; do give it up!' urged the man of the world with the warmth of a lad. 'Come back to England and — '

But the hand he had detained was wrenched from his, and, in the pink sunset sifted through the pines, Stingaree vaulted into his saddle with an oath.

'With a price on my skin!' he cried, and galloped from the gully with a bitter laugh.

And in the moonlight sure enough came bobbing horsemen, with fluttering pugarees and short tunics with silver buttons; but they saw nothing of the missing passenger, who had carried the bags some distance down the road, and had found them quite a comfortable couch in a certain box-clump commanding a sufficient view of the road. Nevertheless, when the little coach came swaying on its leathern springs, its scarlet enamel stained black as ink in the moonshine, he was on the spot to stop it with uplifted arms.

'Don't shoot!' he cried. 'I'm the passenger you put down this afternoon.' And the driver nearly tumbled from his perch.

'What about my mail-bags?' he recovered himself enough to ask: for it was perfectly plain that the pretentiously intrepid passenger had been skulking all day in the scrub, scared by the terrors of the road.

'They're in that clump,' replied Mr. Kentish. 'And you can get them yourself, or send someone else for them, for I have carried them far enough.'

'That be blowed for a yarn!' cried the driver, forgetting his benefits in the virtuous indignation of the moment.

'I don't wonder at your thinking it one,' returned the other, mildly; 'for I never had such absolute luck in all my life!'

And he went on to amplify his first lie like a man.

But when the bags were really back in the coach, piled roof-high on those of the downward mail, then it was worse fun for Guy Kentish outside than even he had anticipated. Question followed question, compliment capped compliment, and a certain unsteady undercurrent of incredulity by no means lessened his embarrassment. Had he but told the truth, he felt he could have borne the praise, and indeed enjoyed it, for he had done far better than anybody was likely to suppose, and already it was irritating to have to keep that circumstance a secret. Yet one thing he was able to say from his soul before the coach drew up at the next stage.

'You should have a spell here,' the driver had suggested, 'and let me pick you up again on my way back. You'd soon lay hands on the bird himself, if you can put salt on his tail as you've done. And no one else can — we want a few more chums like you.'

'I dare say!'

And the new chum's tone bore its own significance.

'You don't mean,' cried the driver, 'to go and tell me you'll hurry home after this?'

'Only by the first steamer!' said Guy Kentish.

And he kept that word as well.

The Taking of Stingaree

Stingaree had crossed the Murray, and all Victoria was agog with the news. It was not his first descent upon that Colony, nor likely to be his last, unless Sub-Inspector Kilbride and his mounted myrmidons did much better than they had done before. There is no stimulus, however, like a trembling reputation. Within four-and-twenty hours Kilbride himself was on the track of the invader, whose heels he had never seen, much less his face. And he rode alone.

It was not merely his reputation that was at stake, though nothing could restore that more effectually than the single-handed capture of so notorious a desperado as Stingaree. The dashing officer was not unnaturally actuated by the sum of three hundred pounds now set upon the outlaw's person, alive or dead. That would be a little windfall for one man, but not much to divide among five or six; on the other hand, and with all his faults, Sub-Inspector Kilbride had courage enough to furnish forth a squadron. He was a black-bearded, high-cheeked Irish-Australian, keen and over-eager to a disease, restless, irascible, but full of the fire and dash that make as dangerous an enemy as another good fighter need desire. And as a fine fighter in an infamous cause, Stingaree had his admirers even in Victoria, where the old tale of popular sympathy with a picturesque rascal was responsible for not the least of the Sub-Inspector's difficulties. But even this struck Kilbride as yet another of those obstacles which were more easily surmounted alone than at the head of a talkative squad; and with that conviction he pushed his thorough-bred on and on through a whole cool night and three parts of an Australian summer's day. Imagine, then, his disgust at the apparition of a mounted trooper galloping to meet him in the middle of the afternoon, and within a few miles of a former hiding-place of the bushranger, where the senior officer had strong hopes of finding and surprising him now.

'Where the devil do you come from?' cried Kilbride, as the other rode up.

'Jumping Creek,' was the crisp reply. 'Stationed there.'

'Then why don't you stop there and do your duty?'

'Stingaree!' said the laconic trooper.

'What! Do you think you're after him too?'

'I am after him.'

'So am I.'

'Then you're going in the wrong direction.'

Kilbride flushed a warm brown from beard to helmet.

'Do you know who you're speaking to?' cried he. 'I'm Sub-Inspector Kilbride, and this business is my business, and no other man's in this Colony. You go back to your barracks, sir! I'm not going to have every damned fool in the force charging about the country on his own account.'

The trooper was a dark, smart, dapper young fellow, of a type not easily browbeaten or subdued. And discipline is not the strong point of forces so irregular as the mounted police of a crescent colony. But nothing could have been more admirable than the manner in which this rebuke was received.

'Very well, sir, if you wish it; but I can assure you that you are off the track of Stingaree.'

'How do *you* know?' asked Kilbride, rudely; but he was beginning to look less black.

'I happen to know the place. You would have some difficulty in finding it if you never were there before. I only stumbled across it by accident myself.'

'Lately?'

'One day last winter when I was out

looking for some horses.'

'And you kept it to yourself!'

The trooper hung his head. 'I knew we should have him across the river again,' he said. 'It was only a question of time; and — well, sir, you can understand!'

'You were keen on taking him yourself, were you?'

'As keen as you are, Mr. Kilbride!' owned the younger man, raising bold eyes, and looking his superior fairly and squarely in the face.

Kilbride returned the stare, and what he saw unsettled him. The other was wiry, trim, eminently alert; he had the masterful mouth and the dare-devil eye, and his horse seemed a part of himself. A more promising comrade at hot work was not to be desired: and the work would be hot if Stingaree had half a chance. After all, it was better for two to succeed than for one to fail. 'Half the money and a whole skin!' said Kilbride to himself, and rapped out his decision with an oath.

The trooper's eyes lit with reckless mirth, and a soft cheer came from under his breath.

'By the bye, what's your name,' said Kilbride, 'before we start?'

'Bowen — Jack Bowen.'

'Then I know all about you! Why on earth didn't you tell me before? It was you who took that black fellow who murdered the shepherd on Woolshed Creek, wasn't it?'

The admission was made with due modesty.

'Why, you're the very man for me!' Kilbride cried. 'You show the way, Jack, and I'll make the going.'

And off they went together at a canter, the slanting sun striking fire from their buttons and accoutrements, and lighting their sun-burnt faces as it lit the red stems and the white that raced past them on either side. For a little they followed the path which Kilbride had taken on his way thither; then the trooper plunged into the thick bush on the left, and the game became follow-my-leader, in and out, out and in, through a maze of red stems and of white, where the pungent eucalyptus scent hung heavy as the sage-green, perpendicular leaves themselves: and so onward until the Sub-Inspector called a halt.

'How far is it now, Bowen?'

'Two or three miles, sir.'

'Good! It'll be light for another hour and a half. We'd better give the mokes a breather while we can. And there'd be no harm in two draws.'

'I was just thinking the same thing, sir.'

So their reins dangled while they cut up a pipeful of apparent shoe-leather apiece: and presently the dull blue smoke was curling and circling against the dull green foliage, producing subtle half-tint harmonies and momentary arabesques as the horses ambled neck and neck.

'Native of this Colony?' puffed Kilbride.

'Well, no — old country originally — but I've been out some years.'

'That's all right so long as you're not a New South Welshman,' said Kilbride, with a chuckle. 'I'll be shot if I wouldn't almost have turned you back if you had been!'

'Victoria is to have all the credit, is she, sir?'

'Anyhow they sha'n't have any on the other side, or I'll know the reason!' the Victorian swore. 'I — I — by Jove, I'd as lief lose my man again as let them have a hand in taking him!'

'But why?'

'Why? Do you live so near the border, and can you ask? Did you never hear a Sydney-side drover blowing about his blooming Colony? Haven't you heard of Sydney Harbor till you're sick? And then their papers!' cried Kilbride, with columns in his tone. 'But I'll have the last laugh yet! I swore I would, and I will! I swore I'd take Stingaree — '

'So I heard.'

'Yes, they put it in their infernal papers!

But it was true — take him I will!'

'Or die in the attempt, eh?'

'Or die and be damned to me!'

All the bitterness of previous failure, indeed of notorious and much-criticized defeat, was in the Sub-Inspector's tone; that of his subordinate, though light as air, had a touch of insolence which an outsider could not have failed — but Kilbride was too excited — to detect. The outsider might possibly have foreseen a rivalry which no longer entered Kilbride's hot head.

Meanwhile the country was changing even with their now leisurely advance. The timbered flats in the region of the river had merged into a gully which was rapidly developing into a gorge, with new luxuriant growths which added greatly to the density of the forest, suggesting its very heart. The almost neutral eucalyptian tint was splashed with the gay hues of many parrots, as though the gum-trees had burst into flower. The noise of running water stole gradually through the murmur of leaves. And suddenly an object in the grass struck the sight like a lantern flashed at dead of night: it proved to be an empty sardine tin pricked by a stray lance from the slanting sun.

'We must be near,' whispered Kilbride.

'We are there! You hear the creek? He has a

gunyah there — that's all. Shall we rush it on horseback or creep up on foot?'

'You know the lie of the land, Bowen; which do you recommend?'

'Rushing it.'

'Then here goes.'

In a few seconds they had leaped their horses into a tiny clearing on the banks of a creek as relatively minute. And the gunyah — a mere funnel of boughs and leaves, in which a man could lie at full length, but only sit upright at the funnel's mouth — seemed as empty as the space on every hand. The only other sign of Stingaree was a hank of rope flung carelessly across the gunyah roof.

'He may be watching us from among the trees,' muttered Kilbride, looking sharply about him. Bowen screwed up his eyes and followed suit.

'I hardly think it, Mr. Kilbride.'

'But it's possible, and here we sit for him to pot us! Let's dismount, whether or no.'

They slid to the ground. The trooper found himself at the mouth of the gunyah.

'What if he were in there after all!' said he.

'He isn't,' said Kilbride, stepping in front and stooping quickly. 'But you might creep in, Jack, and see if he's left any sign of life behind him.'

The men were standing between the

horses, their revolvers cocked. Bowen's answer was to hand his weapon over to Kilbride and to creep into the gunyah on his hands and knees.

'Here's something or other,' his voice cried thickly from within. 'It's half buried. Wait a bit.'

'As sharp as you can!'

'All right; but it's a box, and jolly heavy!'

Kilbride peered nervously to right, left, and centre; then his eyes fell upon his companion wriggling back into the open, a shallow, oblong box in his arms, its polish dimmed and dusted with the mould, as though they had violated a grave.

'Kick it open!' exclaimed Kilbride, excitedly.

But there was no need for that; the box was not even locked; and the lifted lid revealed an inner one of glass, protecting a brass cylinder with steel bristles in uneven growth, and a long line of lilliputian hammers.

'A musical-box!' said the staggered Sub-Inspector.

'That's it, sir. I remember hearing that he'd collared one on one of the stations he stuck up last time he was down here. It must have lain in the ground ever since. And it only shows how hard you must have pressed him, Mr. Kilbride!'

'Yes! I headed him back across the Murray — I soon had him out o' this!' rejoined the other in grim bravado. 'Anything else in the gunyah?'

'All he took that trip, I fancy, if we dig a bit. You never gave him time to roll his swag!'

'I must have a look,' said Kilbride, his excitement fed by his reviving vanity.

The other questioned whether it were worth while. This settled the Sub-Inspector.

'There may be something to show where he's gone,' that casuist suggested, 'for I don't believe he's anywhere here.'

'Shall I hold the shooters, sir?'

'Thanks; and keep your eyes open, just in case. But it's my opinion that the bird's flown somewhere else, and it's for us to find out where.'

Kilbride then crept into the gunyah upon his hands and knees, and found it less dark than he had supposed, the light filtering freely through the leaves and branches. At the inner extremity he found a mildewed blanket, and the place where the musical-box had evidently lain a long time; but there, though he delved to the elbows in the loosened earth, his discoveries ended. Puzzled and annoyed, Kilbride was on the verge of cursing his subordinate, when all at once he was given fresh cause. The musical-box had burst into selections from *The Pirates of Penzance*.

'What the deuce are you at?' shouted the irate officer.

'Only seeing how it goes.'

'Stop it at once, you fool! He may hear it!'

'You said the bird had flown.'

'You dare to argue with me? By thunder, you shall see!'

But it was Sub-Inspector Kilbride who saw most. Backing precipitately out of the gunyah, he turned round before rising upright — and remained upon his knees after all. He was covered by two revolvers — one of them his own — and the face behind the barrels was the one with which the last hour had familiarized Kilbride. The only difference was the single eye-glass in the right eye. And the strains of the musical-box — so thin and tinkling in the open air — filled the pause.

'What in blazes are you playing at?' laughed the luckless officer, feigning to treat the affair as a joke, even while the iron truth was entering his soul by inches.

'Rise another inch without my leave and you may be in blazes to see!'

'Look here, Bowen, what do you mean?'

'Only that Stingaree happens to be at home after all, Mr. Kilbride.'

The victim's grin was no longer forced; the situation made for laughter, even if the laughter were hysterical; and for an instant it was given even to Kilbride to see the cruel humor of it. Then he realized all it meant to him — certain ruin or a sudden death — and the drops stood thick upon his skin.

'What of Bowen?' he at length asked hoarsely. The idea of another victim came as some slight alleviation of his own grotesque case.

'I didn't kill him,' Stingaree.

'Good!' said Kilbride. It was something that two of them should live to share the shame.

'But wing him I did,' added the bushranger. 'I couldn't help myself. The beggar put a bullet through my hat; he did well only to get one back in the leg.'

Kilbride longed to be winged and wounded in his turn, since blood alone could lessen his disgrace. On cooler reflection, however, it was obviously wiser to feign a surrender more abject than it might finally prove to have been.

'Well,' said Kilbride, 'you have the whip-hand over me this time, and I give you best. How long are you going to keep me on my knees?'

'You can get up when you like,' replied Stingaree, 'if you promise not to play the fool. So you were really going to take me this time, were you? I have really no desire to rub it in, but if I were you I should have kept that to myself until I'd done it. And you wanted to have me all to yourself? Well, you couldn't pay me a higher compliment, but I'm going to pay you a high one in return. You really did make me run for it last time, and leave all sorts of things behind. So this time I mean to take them with me and leave you here instead. Nevertheless, you're the only Victorian trap I have any respect for, Mr. Kilbride, or I shouldn't have gone to all this trouble to get you here.'

Kilbride did not blanch, but he heard his apparent doom with a glittering eye, and was deaf for a little to *The Pirates of Penzance*.

'Oh! I'm not going to harm a good man like you,' continued Stingaree, 'unless you make me. Your friend Bowen made me, but I don't promise to fire low every time, mark you! There's another good man on the other side — Cairns by name — you know him, do you? He'll kick up his heels when he hears of this; but they do no better in New South Wales, so don't you let that worry you. To think you held both shooters at one stage of the game! I trusted you, and so you trusted me; if only you had known, eh? Hear that tune, and know what it is? It's in your honor, Mr. Kilbride.'

And Stingaree hummed the policemen's chorus *sotto voce*; but before the end, with a swift remorse, induced by the dignity of Kilbride's bearing in humiliating disaster, he swooped upon the insolent instrument and stopped its tinkle by touching the lever with one revolver-barrel while sedulously covering the Sub-Inspector with the other. The sudden cessation of the toy music, bringing back into undue prominence all the little bush noises which had filled the air before, brought home to Kilbride a position which he had subconsciously associated with those malevolent strains as something theatrical and unreal. He had known in his heart that it was real, without grasping the reality until now. He flung up his fists in sudden entreaty.

'Put a bullet through me,' he cried, 'if you're a man!'

Stingaree shook a decisive head.

'Not if I can help it,' said he. 'But I fear I shall have to tie you up.'

'That's slow death!'

'It never has been yet, but you must take your chance. Get me that rope that's slung over the gunyah. It's got to be done.'

Kilbride obeyed with apparent apathy; but his heart was inflamed with a sudden and infernal glow. Yes, it had never ended in death in any case that he could recall of this time-honored trick of all the bushrangers; on the contrary, sooner or later, most victims had contrived to release themselves. Well, one victim was going to complete his release by hanging himself by the same rope to the same tree! Meanwhile he confronted his captor grimly, the coil in both hands.

'There's a loop at one end,' said Stingaree. 'Stick your foot through it — either foot you like.'

Kilbride obeyed, wondering whether his head would go through when his turn came.

'Now chuck me the other end.'

It fell in coils at the bushranger's feet.

'Now stand up against that blue gum,' he continued, pointing at the tree with Kilbride's revolver, his own being back at his hip. 'And stand still like a sensible chap!'

Stingaree then walked round and round the tree, paying out the long rope, yet keeping it taut, until it wound round tree and man from the latter's ankles to his armpits. Instinctively Kilbride had kept his arms free to the last, but they were no use to him in his suit of hemp, and one after the other his wrists were pinned and handcuffed behind the tree. The cold steel came as a shock. The captive had counted on loosening the knots by degrees, beginning with those about his hands. But there was no loosening steel gyves like these;

he knew the feel of them too well; they were Kilbride's own, that he had brought with him for Stingaree. 'Found 'em in your saddle-bags while you were in my gunyah,' explained the bushranger, stepping round to survey his handiwork. 'Sorry to scar the kid — so to speak! But you see you were my most dangerous enemy on this side of the Murray!'

The enemy did not look very dangerous as he stood in the dusk, in the heart of that forest, lashed to that tree, with his finger-tips not quite meeting behind it, and the blood already on his wrists.

'And now?' he whispered, hoarse already, his lips cracking, and his throat parched.

'I shall give you a drink before I go.'

'I won't take one from you!'

'I shall make you, if I have to be a bigger brute than ever. You must live to spin this yarn!'

'Never!'

Stingaree smiled to himself as he produced pipe and tobacco; but it was not his sinister smile; it was rather that of the victor who salutes the vanquished in his heart. Meanwhile a more striking and a more subtle change had come over the face of Kilbride. It was not joy, but it was quite a new grimness, and in his own preoccupation the bushranger did not notice it at all. He sauntered nearer with his knife and his tobacco-plug, and there was some compassion in his pensive stare.

'Cheer up, man!' said he. 'There's no disgrace in coming out second best to me. You may smile. You'll find it's generally admitted in New South Wales. And after all, you needn't tell little crooked Cairns how it happened. So that stops your smile! But he's the best man left on my tracks, and I shouldn't be surprised if he's the first to find you.'

'No more should I!' said a harsh voice behind the bushranger. 'Hands up and empty, Stingaree, or you're the next dead man in this little Colony!'

Quick as thought Stingaree stepped in front of the tied Victorian. But his hands were up, and his eye-glass dangling on its string.

'Oh, you don't catch me kill two birds,' rasped the newcomer's voice, 'though I'm not sure which of you would be least loss!'

Stingaree stood aside once more, and waved his hands without lowering them, bowing from his captor to his captive as he did so.

'Superintendent Cairns, of New South Wales — Inspector Kilbride, of Victoria,' said he. 'You two men will be glad to know each other.'

The New South Welshman drawled out a

dry expression of his own satisfaction. His was a strange and striking personality. Dark as a mulatto, and round-shouldered to the extent of some distinct deformity, he carried his eyes high under the lids, and shot his piercing glance from under the penthouse of a beetling brow; a lipless mouth was pursed in such a fashion as to shorten the upper lip and exaggerate an already powerful chin; and this stooping and intent carriage was no less suggestive of the human sleuth-hound than were the veiled vigilance and dogged determination of the lowered face. Such was the man who had succeeded where Kilbride had failed — succeeded at the most humiliating moment of that most ignominious failure — and who came unwarrantably from the wrong side of the Murray. The Victorian stood in his bonds and favored his rival with such a glare as he had not levelled at Stingaree himself. But not a syllable did Kilbride vouchsafe. And the Superintendent was fully occupied with his prisoner.

"'Little crooked Cairns,' am I? There are those that look a jolly sight smaller, and'll have a worse hump than mine for the rest of their born days! Come nearer and turn your back.'

And the revolver was withdrawn from its carrier on the stolen constabulary belt. The bushranger was then searched for other weapons; then marched into the bush at the pistol's point, and brought back handcuffed to the Superintendent's bridle.

'That's the way you'll come marching home, my boy; and one of us on horseback each side; don't trust *you* in a saddle on a dark night!'

Indeed, it was nearly dark already, and in the nebulous middle-distance a laughing jackass was indulging in his evening peal. Cairns jerked his head in the direction of the unearthly cackle. 'Lots of 'em down here in Vic, I believe,' said he, and at length turned his attention to the bound man. 'You see, I wanted to land him alive and kicking without spilling blood,' he continued, opening his knife. 'That was why I had to let him tie you up.'

'You *let* him?' thundered the Victorian, breaking his silence with a bellow. It was as though the man with the knife had cut through the rope into the bound man's body.

'Stand still,' said he, 'or I may hurt you. I had to let him, my good fellow, or we'd have been dropping each other like bullocks. As it is, not a scratch between us, though I found young Bowen in a pretty bad way. Our friend had stuck up Jumping Creek barracks in the small hours, put a bullet through Bowen's leg, and come away in his uniform. Pretty tall, that, eh? I shouldn't wonder if you'd swing him for it alone, down here in Vic; no doubt you've got to be more severe in a young Colony. Well, I tracked my gentleman to the barracks, and I found Bowen in his blood, sent my trooper for a doctor, and got on *your* tracks before they were half an hour old. I came up with you just as he'd stuck you up. He had one in each hand. It wasn't quite good enough at the moment.'

The knife shore through the rope for the last time, and it lay in short ends all round the tree.

'Now my hands,' cried Kilbride fiercely.

'I beg pardon?' said the satirical Superintendent.

'My hands, I tell you!'

'There's a little word they teach 'em to say at our State Schools. Perhaps you never heard it down in Vic?'

'Don't be a silly fool,' said Kilbride, wearily. 'You haven't been through what I have!'

'That's true,' said Cairns. 'Still, you might be decently civil to the man that gets you out of a mess.'

Nevertheless, the handcuffs were immediately removed; and that instant, with the curtest thanks, Sub-Inspector Kilbride sprang forward with such vigorous intent that the other detained him forcibly by one of his stiff and aching arms.

'What are you after now, Kilbride?'

'My prisoner!'

'Your what?'

'*My* prisoner,' I said.

'I like that — and you his!'

Kilbride burst into a voluble defence of his position.

'What right have you on this side of the Murray, you Sydney-sider? None at all, except as a passenger. You can't lay finger on man, woman, or child in this Colony, and, by God, you sha'n't! Nor yet upon the three hundred there's on his head; and the sons of convicts down in Sydney can put *that* in their pipe and smoke it!'

For all his cool and ready insolence, the misshapen Superintendent from the other side stood dazed and bewildered by this volcanic outpouring. Then his dark face flushed darker, and with a snarl he clinched his fists. The Victorian, however, had turned on his heel, and now his liberated hands flew skyward, as though the bushranger's revolver covered him yet again.

But there was no such weapon discernible through the shade; no New South Welshman's horse; and neither sight, sound, wraith, nor echo of Stingaree, the outlawed bushranger, the terror and the despair of the Sister Colonies!

'I thought it might be done when I saw how you fixed him,' said Kilbride cheerfully. 'Those beggars can ride lying down or standing up!'

'I believe you saw him clear!'

'I'll settle that with you when I've caught him.'

'You catch him, you gum-sucker, when you as good as let him go!'

And a volley of further and far more trenchant abuse was discharged by Superintendent Cairns, of the New South Wales Police. But Kilbride was already in the saddle; a covert outward kick with his spurred heel, and the third horse went cantering riderless into the trees.

'He won't go far,' sang the Sub-Inspector, 'and he'll take you safe back to barracks if you give him his head. It's easy to get bushed in this country — for new chums from penal settlements!'

As the Victorian galloped into the darkness, and the New South Welshman dashed wildly after the third horse, the laughing jackass in the invisible middle-distance gave his last grotesque guffaw at departed day. And the laughing jackass is a Victorian bird.

The Honor of the Road

Sergeant Cameron was undressing for bed when he first heard the voices through the weather-board walls; in less than a minute there was a knock at his door.

'Here's Mr. Hardcastle from Rosanna, sir. He says he must see you at once.'

'The deuce he does! What about?'

'He says he'll only tell you; but he's ridden over in three hours, and he looks like the dead.'

'Give him some whiskey, Tyler, and tell him I'll be down in two ticks.'

So saying, the gray-bearded sergeant of the New South Wales Mounted Police tucked his night-gown into his cord breeches, slipped into his tunic, and hastened to the parlor which served as court-room on occasion, buttoning as he went. Mr. Hardcastle had a glass to his lips as the sergeant entered. He was a very fine man of forty, and his massive frame was crowned with a countenance as handsome as it was open and bold; but at a glance it was plain that he was both shaken and exhausted, and in no mood to hide either his fatigue or his distress. Sergeant Cameron sat down on the other side of the oval table with the faded cloth; the younger constable had left the room when Hardcastle called him back.

'Don't go, Tyler,' said he. 'You may as well both hear what I've got to say. It's — it's Stingaree!'

The name was echoed in incredulous undertones.

'But he's down in Vic,' urged the sergeant. 'He's been giving our chaps a devil of a time down there!'

'He's come back. I've seen him with my own eyes. But I'm beginning at the wrong end first,' said the squatter, taking another sip and then sitting back to survey his hearers. 'You know old Duncan, my overseer?'

The sergeant nodded.

'Of course you know him,' the other continued, 'and so does the whole back-country, and did even before he won this fortune in the Melbourne Cup sweep. I suppose you've heard how he took the news? He was fuddling himself from his own bottle on Sunday afternoon when the mail came; the first I knew of it was when I saw him sitting with his letter in one hand and throwing out the rest of his grog with the other. Then he told us he had won the first prize of thirty thousand, and that he had made up his mind to have his next drink at his own place in Scotland. He left us that afternoon to catch the coach and go down to Sydney for his money. He ought to have been back this evening before sundown.'

The sergeant put in his word:

'That he ought, for I saw him come off the coach and start for the station as soon as they'd run up the horse he left behind him at the pub. I wondered what had brought him, if he was so set on getting back to the old country.'

'I could tell you,' said Hardcastle, after some little hesitation, 'and I may as well. Poor old Duncan was the most generous of men, and nothing would serve him but that every soul on Rosanna should share more or less in his good fortune. I am ashamed to tell you how much he spoke of pressing on myself. You have probably heard that one of his peculiarities was that he would never take payment by check, like other people? I believe it was because he had knocked down too many checks in his day. In any case, we used to call him Hard Cash Duncan on Rosanna; and I am very much afraid that when you saw him he must have had the whole of his thirty thousand pounds upon him in the hardest form of cash.'

'But what has happened, Mr. Hardcastle?'

'The very worst,' said Hardcastle, stooping to sip. The three heads came closer together across the faded tablecloth. 'There was no sign of him at seven; he ought to have been with us before six. We had done our best to make it an occasion, and it seemed that the dinner would be spoilt. So at seven young Evans, my storekeeper, went off at a gallop to meet him, and at twenty-five past he came galloping back leading a riderless horse. It was the one you saw Duncan riding this afternoon. There was blood upon the saddle. I found it. And within another hour we had found the poor old boy himself, dead and cold in the middle of the track, with a bullet through his heart.'

The squatter's voice trembled with an emotion that did him honor in his hearers' eyes; and the gray-bearded sergeant waited a little before asking questions.

'What makes you think it is Stingaree?' he inquired, at length.

'I tell you I saw him on the run, with my own eyes, this morning. I passed him in one of my paddocks, as close as I am to you, and asked him if he was looking for the homestead. He answered that he was only riding through, and we neither of us stopped.'

'Yet you knew all the time that it was Stingaree?'

'No; to be quite honest,' replied Hard-castle, 'I never dreamt of it at the time. But now I am quite positive on the point. He hadn't his eye-glass in his eye, but it was dangling on its cord all right; and there was the curled mustache, and the boots and breeches that one knows all about, if one has never seen them for oneself. Yet I own it didn't dawn on me just then. I happened to be thinking of the stations round about, and wondering if they were as burnt up as we are, and when I met this swell I simply took him for a new chum on one or other of them.'

'There had been robbery, of course?'

'An absolute clearance,' said Hardcastle. 'The valise had been cut to ribbons with a knife, and its other contents were strewed all about; a pocketbook we found still bulging from the roll of notes which had been taken out. I waited beside him while Evans went back for the buggy, and when they started to take him in I rode on to you.'

'We'll ride back with you at once,' said the sergeant, 'and find you a fresh horse if your own has had enough. Run up the lot, Tyler, and Mr. Hardcastle can take his choice. It seems clear enough,' continued Cameron, as the trooper disappeared. 'But this is a new departure for Stingaree; it's the very thing that everybody said he would never do.'

'And yet it's the logical climax of his career; it might have happened long ago, but it's not his first blood as it is,' argued Hardcastle, when he had drained his glass. 'Didn't he wing one of you down in Victoria the other day? Your bushranger is bound to come to it sooner or later. He may much prefer not to shoot; but he has only to get up against a man of his own calibre, as resolute and as well armed as himself, to have no choice in the matter. Poor old Duncan was the very type; he would never have given way. In fact, we found him with his own revolver fast in his hand, and a finger frozen to the trigger, but not a chamber discharged.'

'Yes? Then that settles it, and it must have been foul play,' cried Cameron, owning a doubt in its dismissal. 'And we mustn't lose a single minute in getting on this blackguard's tracks.'

Yet it was midnight before the little cavalcade set out upon a ride of over thirty miles, for arrangements had to be made for a telegram to be sent to the Glenranald coroner first thing in the morning, and to insure this it was necessary to disturb the postmaster, who occupied one of the three weather-board dwellings which constituted the roadside hamlet of Clear Corner. A round moon topped the sand-hills as the trio rode away; it

145

was near its almost dazzling zenith when they reined up at the scene of the murder. This was at a point where the sandy track ran through a belt of scrub, and the sergeant got off to examine the ground with Hardcastle, while Tyler mounted guard in the saddle. But nothing of importance was discovered by the pair on foot, and nothing seen or heard by their mounted comrade.

They found the station still astir and faintly aglow in the veiled daylight of the moon. A cluster of the men stood in a glare at the door of their hut; the travellers' hut betrayed the like symptoms of excitement; at the kitchen door were more men with pannikins, and odd glimpses of a firelit, white-capped face within. But on the broad veranda sat two young men with their backs to a closed and darkened window. And behind the window lay all that remained of an elderly man, whose brown, gnarled face was scarcely recognizable by the newcomers in its strange smooth pallor, but his grizzled beard weirdly familiar and still crisp with lingering life.

The coroner arrived in some thirty hours, which had brought forth nothing new; his jury was drawn from the men's hut and rabbiters' tents; and after a prolonged but inconclusive investigation, the inquest was adjourned for a week. But the seven days were as barren as the first, and a verdict against some person unknown a foregone result. This did not satisfy the many who were positive that they knew the person; for Stingaree had been seen a hundred miles lower down, doubtless on his way back to Victoria, and with his appearance altered in a telltale manner. But the coroner thought he knew better than anybody else, and had his way, notwithstanding the manifest feeling on the long veranda where he held his court.

So jurors and spectators drifted back to hut and tent and neighboring station, the coroner started in his buggy for Glenranald, and last of all the police departed, leading the horse which Hardcastle had ridden home from their barracks, and leaving him at peace once more with his two young men. But on the squatter the time had told; his table had been full to overflowing through it all; and he sank into a long chair, a trifle grayer at the temples, a thought looser in his dress, as the pugarees of Cameron and Tyler fluttered out of sight.

'I think we might have a drink,' he said with a wry smile to Evans, who fetched the decanter from the store; the jackeroo was called from a stable which had become Augean during the week, and the three were still mildly tippling when the store-keeper came to his feet.

'Good Lord!' cried he. 'I thought we'd seen the last of the plucky police!'

'You don't mean to say they're coming back?'

'I do, worse luck! Cameron, Tyler, and some new joker in plain clothes.'

Hardcastle finished his drink with a resigned smile, and stood on the veranda to receive the intruders.

'After all, it will stave off the reaction I began to feel the moment they had turned their backs,' said he. 'Well, well, well! I thought I'd just got rid of you fellows, and back you come like base coin!'

'You mustn't blame us,' said the sergeant, first to dismount. 'We couldn't know that Superintendent Cairns had been sent up from Sydney, much less that we should ride right into him in your horse-paddock!'

The squatter had stepped down from the veranda with polite alacrity.

'Glad to see you, Mr. Cairns,' said he. 'I only wish you had come before.'

The creature in the plain clothes looked about him with a dry smile, and a sharp eye upon the younger men and the empty glasses, as he and the sergeant accompanied Hardcastle to the veranda, while Tyler took charge of the three horses. The fame of Cairns had travelled before him to Rosanna, but none had been prepared for a figure so weird or for a countenance so forbidding and malign. His manners were equally uncouth. He shook his bent head to decline refreshment; he pointedly ignored a generalization of Hard-castle's about the crime; and when he spoke, it was in a gratuitously satirical style of his own.

'May I ask, Mr. Hardcastle, if you are the owner or the manager of this lodge in a howling wilderness?'

'I'm sorry to say I am both.'

'I appreciate the sorrow. I failed to discern a single green blade as I came along.'

'We depend on salt-bush and the like.'

'In spite of which, I believe, you have had several lean years?'

'There's no denying it.'

'I am sorry to be one of so many intruders in such a season, Mr. Hardcastle, but I shall not trouble you long. I hope to take the murderer to-night.'

'Stingaree?'

'Not quite so loud, please. Who else, should you suppose? You may be interested to hear that he has been in hiding on your run for several days, and so have I, within fairly easy reach of him. But he is not a man to be taken single-handed without further loss of life; so I intercepted you, sergeant, and now you are both enlightened. To-night, with your assistance and that of your young colleague, I count upon a bloodless victory. But I should prefer you, Mr. Hardcastle, not to mention the matter to the very young men whom I noticed in your company on my arrival. Have I your promise to comply with my wishes on this point, and on any other which may arise in connection with the capture?'

And a steely glitter shot through the beetling eyebrows; but Hardcastle had given his word before the request was rounded to that pedantic neatness which characterized the crabbed utterances of the round-shouldered dictator.

'That is well,' he went on, 'for now I can admit you both into my plan of campaign. Suppose we sit down here on the veranda, at the end farthest from any door. Be good enough to draw your chairs nearer mine, gentlemen. It might be dangerous if a fourth person heard me say that I had discovered the murderer's ill-gotten hoard!'

'Not you, sir!' cried Cameron.

'Good God!' exclaimed the squatter.

'The discoverer was not divine, and indeed no human being but myself,' the bent man averred, turning with mischievous humor from one to the other of his astonished hearers. 'Yes, there was more gold than I would have credited a sane Scotchman with carrying through the wilds; but the bulk was in small notes and the whole has been buried in the scrub close to the scene of the murder, doubtless to avoid at once the detection and the division of such unusual spoil.'

'You are thinking of his mate?'

It was Cameron who had asked the question, but Mr. Hardcastle followed immediately with another.

'Did you remove the spoil?'

'My dear Mr. Hardcastle! How you must lack the detective instinct! Of course, I left everything as nearly as possible as I found it; the man camps on the spot, or very near it; he lights no fires and is careful to leave no marks, but I am more or less convinced of it. And that is where I shall take him to-night, or, rather, early tomorrow morning.'

'I wish you could make it to-night,' said Hardcastle, with a yawn that put a period to a pause of some duration.

'Why?' demanded the detective, raising open eyes for once.

'Because I've had a desperate week of it,' replied Hardcastle, 'and am dead with sleep.'

The other carried his growing geniality to the length of an almost hearty laugh.

'My dear sir, do you suppose that I thought of taking *you* with us? No, Mr. Hardcastle, the risks of this sort of enterprise are for those who are paid to run them. And there is a risk; if we timed our attack too early or too late there would be bloodshed to a certainty. But at two o'clock the average man is fast asleep; at a quarter after one, therefore, I start with Sergeant Cameron and Constable Tyler.'

Hardcastle yawned again.

'I should like to have been with you, but there are compensations,' said he. 'I doubt if I shall even stay up to see you off.'

'If you did you would sit up alone,' returned the Superintendent. 'I intend to turn in myself for three or four hours; and it will be in the face of all my wishes, sergeant, if you and Tyler do not do the same. No reason to tell him what a short night it's to be; it might prevent a young fellow like that from getting any sleep at all. Merely let it be arranged that we all turn in betimes in view of an early start; we three alone need know how early the start will be.'

They had their simple dinner at half-past seven, when the detective took it on himself to entertain the party, and succeeded so well that the entertainment was continued on the veranda for the better part of another hour. Doubled up in his chair, abnormal, weird, he recounted in particular the exploits of Stingaree (included a garbled version of the recent fiasco across the Murray) with a zest only equalled by his confidant undertaking to avenge the death of Robert Duncan before another day was out; all listened in a rapt silence, and the younger men were duly disappointed when the party broke up prematurely between nine and ten. But they also had played their part in a fatiguing week; by the later hour all were in their rooms, and before very long Rosanna Station lay lighted only by the full white moon of New South Wales.

Cameron wondered if it could possibly be two o'clock, while Tyler sat up insensate with the full weight of his first sleep, when their chief crept into the double-bedded room in which the two policemen had been put. He owned himself before his time by an hour and more, but explained that he had an idea which had only struck him as he was about to fall asleep.

'If we hunt for the fellow in the dark,' said he, 'we may give him the alarm before we come on him. But if we go now there is at least a chance that we may find his fire to guide us. I am aware I said he wouldn't light one there, but everybody knows that Stinga-ree uses a spirit-lamp. In any case it's a chance, and with a desperate man like that we can't afford to give the ghost of a chance away.'

The sergeant dressed without more ado, as did his subordinate on learning the nature of their midnight errand; meanwhile the disturber of slumbers was gone to the horse-yard to start saddling. The others followed in a few minutes. And there was the horse-yard overflowing with moonshine, but empty alike of man and beast.

'I wonder what's got him?' murmured the bewildered sergeant uneasily.

'Old Harry, for all I care!' muttered the other. 'I'm no such nuts on him, if you ask me. There's a bit too much of him for my taste.'

In his secret breast the sergeant entertained a similar sentiment, but he was too old an officer to breathe disaffection in the ear of his subaltern. He contented himself with a mild expression of his surprise at the conduct of the Sydney authorities in putting a 'towny' over his head without so much as a word of notice.

'And such a 'towny'!' echoed Tyler. 'One you never heard of in your life before, and never will again!'

'Speak for yourself!' rejoined Cameron, irritated at the exaggeration of their case. 'I have heard of him ever since I joined the force.'

'Well, he's a funny joke to have shoved over us, a blooming little hunchback like that.'

'I always heard that he was none the worse for what he couldn't help, and now I can understand it,' said the sergeant, 'for he's not such a hunch — '

The men looked at each other in the moonlight, and the ugly word was never finished. A dozen hoofs were galloping upon them, their thunder muffled by the sandy road, and into the tank of moonshine came two horses, hounded by the detective bareback on the third.

'Someone left the slip-rails down, and they were all over the horse-paddock,' he panted. 'But I took a bridle and managed to catch one, and it was easy enough to run up the other two.'

But even Constable Tyler thought the more of their misshapen leader for the feat.

There was now no time to be lost, for it approached midnight, but the trio were soon cantering through the horse-paddock neck-and-neck, and the new day found them at the farther gate. The moon still poured unbroken brilliance upon that desert world of sandy stretches tufted with salt-bush and erratically overgrown with scrub. The shadow of the gate was as another gate lying ready to be hung; for each particular wire in the fence there was a thin black stripe upon the ground. The three passed through, and came in quick time upon the edge of that scrub in which the crime had been committed. And here the chief called a halt.

'The two to nail him must be on foot,' said he. 'You can creep upon him on foot as you never could with a horse; but I will remain mounted in the road and ride him down if he shows fight.'

So the pair in the pugarees walked one at either stirrup of their crooked chief, leaving the two horses tethered to a tree, until of a sudden the whole party halted as one. They had rounded a bend in the road with great caution, for they all knew where they were; but only one of them was prepared for the position of the light which flashed into their eyes from the heart of the scrub.

It was a tiny light, set low upon the ground, and yet it flashed through the forest like a diamond in a bundle of hay. It burnt at no little distance from the track, for at a movement it was lost, but it was some hundreds of yards nearer the station than the scene of the murder. The chief whispered that this was where he had found the buried booty, and over half the distance he led the way, winding in and out among the trees, now throwing a leg across his horse's withers to avoid a hole, anon embracing its neck to escape contact with the branches. It was long before they could discern anything but the light itself amid the trunks and branches of the scrub.

Suddenly the horseman stopped, beckoning with his free hand to the pair afoot, pointing at the fire with the one that held the reins; and as they crept up to him he stooped in the stirrups till his mouth was close to the sergeant's ear.

'He's sitting on the far side of the light, but you can't see his face. I thought he was a log, and I still believe he's asleep. Creep on him like cats till he looks up; then rush him with your revolvers before he can draw his, and I'll support you with mine!'

Nearer and nearer stole Cameron and Tyler; the rider managed to coax a few more noiseless steps from his clever mount, but dropped the reins and squared his elbows some twenty paces from the light — a hurricane lamp now in the sharpest focus. The policemen crawled some yards ahead; all three carried revolver in hand. But still the unsuspecting figure sat motionless, his chin upon his chest, the brim of his wideawake hiding his face, a little heap of gold and notes before him on the ground. Then the Superintendent's horse flung up its head; its teeth champed upon the bit; the man sat bolt upright, and the light of the hurricane lamp fell full upon the face of Hardcastle the squatter.

'Rush him! rush him! That's the man we want!'

But the momentary stupefaction of the police had given Hardcastle his opportunity; the hurricane lamp flew between them, going out where it fell, and for a minute the revolvers spat harmlessly in the remaining patchwork of moonshine and shadow.

'Get behind trees; shoot low, don't kill him!' shouted the chief from his saddle. 'Now on to him before he can load again. That's it! Pin him! Throw your revolvers away, or he'll snatch one before you know where you are! Ah, I thought he was too strong for you! Mr. Hardcastle, I'll put a bullet through you myself if you don't instantly surrender!'

And the fight ended with the bent man leaning in his stirrups over the locked and swaying group, as he brandished his revolver to suit deed to word. It was a heavy blow with the long barrel that finally turned the scale. In a few seconds Hardcastle stood a prisoner, the handcuffs fitting his large wrists like gloves, his great frame panting from the fray, and yet a marvel of monstrous manhood in its stoical and defiant carriage.

'For God's sake, Cairns, do what you say!' he cried. 'Put three bullets through me, and divide what's on the ground between you!'

'I half wish we could, for your sake,' was the reply. 'But it's idle to speak of it, and I'm afraid you've committed a crime that places you beyond the reach of sympathy.'

'That he has!' cried the sergeant, wiping blood from his gray beard. 'It's plain as a pikestaff now; and to think that he was the one to come and fetch us the very night he'd done it! But what licks me more than anything is how in the world you found him out, sir!'

The hunchback looked down upon the stalwart prisoner standing up to his last inch between his two captors: there was an impersonal interest in the man's bold eyes that invited a statement more eloquently than the sergeant's tongue.

'I will tell you,' said the horseman, smiling down upon the three on foot. 'In the first place, I had my own reasons for knowing that Stingaree was nowhere near this place on the night of the murder, for I happen to have been on his tracks for some time. Who knew all about the dead man's stroke of luck, his insane preference for hard cash, the time of his return? Mr. Hardcastle, for one. Who swore that he had met Stingaree face to face upon the run? Mr. Hardcastle alone; there was not a soul to corroborate or contradict him. Who was in need of many thousand pounds? Mr. Hardcastle, as I suspected, and as he practically admitted to me when we discussed the bad season on my arrival. I was pretty sure of my man before I crossed the boundary fence, but I was absolutely convinced before I had spent twenty minutes on his veranda.'

The prisoner smiled sardonically in the moonlight. The policemen gazed with awe upon the man who had solved a nine days' mystery in fewer hours.

'You must remember,' he continued, 'that I have spent some days and nights upon the run; during the days I have camped in the thickest scrub I could find, but by night I have been very busy, and last night I had a stroke of luck. I stumbled by accident on a track that led me to the place I had been looking for all along. You see, I had put myself in Hardcastle's skin, and I was quite clear that I should have buried a lapful of gold and notes somewhere in the bush until the hue and cry had blown over. Not that I expected to find it so near the scene of the crime — I should certainly have gone farther afield myself.'

'But I can't make out why that wasn't enough for you, sir,' ventured the sergeant, deferentially. 'Why didn't you come in and arrest him on that?'

'You shall see in three minutes. Wasn't it far better to catch him red-handed as we have? You will at least admit that it was far neater. I say I have the place. I say we are all going to it at two in the morning. I say, let us sleep till a little after one. Was it not obvious what would happen? The only thing I did not expect was to find him asleep with the swag under his nose.'

Then Hardcastle spoke up.

'I was not asleep,' said he. 'I thought I was safe for an hour or two . . . and I began to think . . . I was wondering what to do . . . whether to cut my throat at once . . . '

And his dreadful voice died away like a single chord struck in an empty room.

'But Stingaree,' put in Tyler in the end. 'What's happened to him?'

'He also has been here. But he was many a mile away at the time.'

'What brought him here?'

The crooked Superintendent from Sydney was sitting strangely upright in his saddle; his face was not to be seen, for his back was to the moon, but he seemed to rub one of his eyes.

'He may have wished to clear his character. He may have itched to uphold the honor of that road of which he considers himself a not imperfect knight. He may have found it so jolly easy to play policeman down in Victoria, that he couldn't resist another shot in a better cause up here. At his worst he never killed a man in all his life. And you will be good enough to take his own word for it that he never will!'

He had backed his horse while he spoke; he turned a little to the light, and the eyeglass gleamed in his eye.

The young constable sprang forward.

'Stingaree!' he screamed.

But the gray sergeant flung his arms round their prisoner.

'That's right!' cried the bushranger, as he trotted off. 'Your horses and even your pistols are out of reach, thanks to a discipline for which I love you dearly. You hang on to your bird in the hand, my friends, and never again misjudge the one in the bush!'

And as the trees swallowed the cantering horse and man, followed by a futile shot from the first revolver which the young constable had picked up, an embittered admiration kindled in the captive murderer's eyes.

The Purification of Mulfera

Mulfera Station, N.S.W., was not only an uttermost end of the earth, but an exceedingly loose end, and that again in more senses than one. There were no ladies on Mulfera, and this wrought inevitable deterioration in the young men who made a bachelors' barracks of the homestead. Not that they ever turned it into the perfect pandemonium you might suppose; but it was unnecessary either to wear a collar or to repress an oath at table; and this sort of disregard does not usually stop at the elementary decencies. It is true that on Mulfera the bark of the bachelor was something worse than his bite, and his tongue no fair criterion to the rest of him. Nevertheless, the place became a byword, even in the back-blocks; and when at last the good Bishop Methuen had the hardihood to include it in an episcopal itinerary, there were admirers of that dear divine who roundly condemned his folly, and enemies who no longer denied his heroism.

The Lord Bishop of the Back-Blocks had at that time been a twelvemonth or more in charge of what he himself described playfully as his 'oceanic see'; but his long neglect of Mulfera was due less to its remoteness than to the notorious fact that they wanted no adjectival and alliterative bishops there. An obvious way of repulse happened to be open to the blaspheming squatter, though there is no other instance of its employment. On these up-country visitations the Bishop was dependent for his mobility upon the horse-flesh of his hospitable hosts; thus it became the custom to send to fetch him from one station to another; and as a rule the owner or the manager came himself, with four horses and the big trap. The manager of Mulfera said his horses had something else to do, and his neighbors backed him up with some discreet encouragement on their own account. It was felt that a slur would be left upon the whole district if his lordship actually met with the only sort of reception which was predicted for him on Mulfera. Bishop Methuen, however, was one of the last men on earth to shirk a plague-spot; and on this one, warning was eventually received that the Bishop and his chaplain would arrive on horseback the following Sunday morning, to conduct divine service, if quite convenient, at eleven o'clock.

The language of the manager was something inconceivable upon the receipt of this cool advice. He was a man named Carmichael, and quite a different type from the neighbors who held up horny hands when the Bishop decided on his raid. Carmichael was not 'a native of this colony,' or of the next, but he was that distressing spectacle, the public-school man who is no credit to his public school. Worse than this, he was a man of brains; worst of all, he had promised very differently as a boy. A younger man who had been at school with him, having come out for his health, travelled some hundreds of miles to see Carmichael, whose conversation struck him absolutely dumb. 'He was captain of our house,' the visitor explained to Carmichael's subordinates, 'and you daren't say dash in dormitory — not even dash!'

In appearance this redoubtable person was chiefly remarkable for the intellectual cast of his still occasionally clean-shaven countenance, and for his double eyeglasses, or rather the way he wore them. They were very strong and very common, without any rims, and Carmichael bought them by the box. He would not wear them with a cord, and in the heat they were continually slipping off his nose; when they did not slip right off they hung at such an angle that Carmichael had to throw his whole body and head backward in order to see anything through them except the ground. And when they fell, someone else had to find them while Carmichael cursed, for his naked eye was as blind as a bat's.

'Let's go mustering on Sunday,' suggested the overseer — 'every blessed man! Let him find the whole place deserted, homestead and hut!'

'Or let's get blind for the occasion,' was the bookkeeper's idea — 'every mother's son!'

'That would do,' agreed the overseer, 'if we got just blind enough. And we might get the blacks from Poonee Creek to come and join the dance.'

The overseer was a dapper Victorian with a golden mustache twisted rakishly up and down at either end respectively, like an overturned letter S. He lived up to the name of Smart. The bookkeeper was a servile echo with a character and a face of putty. He had once perpetrated an opprobrious ode to the overseer, and had answered to the name of Chaucer ever since.

Carmichael leaned back to look from one of these worthies to the other, and his spectacled eyes flamed with mordant scorn.

'I suppose you think you're funny, you fellows,' said he, and without the oath which was a sign of his good-will, except when he lost his temper with the sheep. 'If so, I wish you'd get outside to entertain each other.

166

Since the fellow's coming we shall have to let him come, and the thing is how to choke him off ever coming again without open insult, which I won't allow. A service of some sort we shall have to have, this once.'

'I'm on to guy it,' declared the indiscreet Chaucer.

'If you do I'll rehearse the men,' the overseer promised.

'You idiots!' thundered Carmichael, whose temper was as short as his sight. 'Can't you see I weaken on the prospect as much as the two of you stuck together? But the beggar's certain to be a public-school and 'Varsity man: and I won't have him treated as though he'd been dragged up in one of these God-forsaken Colonies!'

Now — most properly — you cannot talk like this in the bush unless you are also capable of confirming the insult with your fists. But Carmichael could; and he was much too blind to fight without his glasses. He was, in fact, the same strenuous character who had set his dogmatic face against the most harmless expletives in dormitory at school, and set it successfully, because Carmichael was a mighty man, whose influence was not to be withstood. His standard alone was changed. Or he was playing on the other side. Yet he had brought a prayer-book with him to the back-blocks. And he was seen studying it on the eve of the episcopal descent.

'He may have his say,' observed Carmichael, darkly, 'and then I'll have mine.'

'Going to heckle him?' inquired Smart, in a nasal voice full of hope and encouragement.

'Not at the function, you fool,' replied Carmichael, sweetly. 'But when it's all over I should like to take him on about the Athanasian Creed and the Thirty-nine Articles.' Only both substantives were qualified by the epithet of the country, for Carmichael had put himself in excellent temper for the day of battle.

That day dawned blood-red and beautiful, but in a little it was a blinding blue from pole to pole, and the thermometer in the veranda reached three figures before breakfast. It was a hot-wind day, and even Carmichael's subordinates pitied Dr. Methuen and his chaplain, who were riding from the south in the teeth of that Promethean blast. But Carmichael himself drew his own line with unswerving rigidity; and though the deep veranda was prepared as a place for worship, and covered in with canvas which was kept saturated with water, he would not permit an escort to sally even to the boundary fence to meet the uninvited prelate.

Not long after breakfast the two horsemen

jogged into view, ambling over the sand-hills whose red-hot edge met a shimmering sky some little distance beyond the station pines. Both wore pith helmets and fluttering buff dust-coats, but both had hot black legs, the pair in gaiters being remarkable for their length. The homestead trio, their red necks chafed by the unaccustomed collar, gathered grimly at the open end of the veranda, where they exchanged impressions while the religious raiders bore down upon them.

'They can ride a bit, too, I'm bothered if they can't,' exclaimed the overseer, in considerable astonishment.

'And do you suppose, my good fool,' inquired Carmichael, with the usual unregenerate embroidery — 'do you in your innocence suppose that's an accomplishment confined to these precious provinces?'

'They're as brown as my sugar,' said the keeper of books and stores.

'The Bishop looks as though he'd been out here all his life.'

Carmichael did not quarrel with this observation of his overseer, but colorless eyebrows were raised above the cheap glasses as he stepped into the yard to shake hands with the visitors. The bearded Bishop returned his greeting in a grave silence. The chaplain, on the other hand, seemed the victim of a nervous volubility, and unduly anxious to atone for his chief's taciturnity, which he essayed to explain to Carmichael on the first opportunity.

'His lordship feels the heat so much more than I do, who have had so many years of it; and to tell you the truth, he is still a little hurt at not being met, for the first time since he has been out here.'

'Then why did he come?' demanded Carmichael, bluntly. 'I never asked him, did I?'

'No, no, but — ah, well! We won't go into it,' said the chaplain. 'I am glad to see your preparations, Mr. Carmichael; that I consider very magnanimous in you, under all the circumstances; and so will his lordship when he has had a rest. You won't mind his retiring until it's time for the little service, Mr. Carmichael?'

'Not I,' returned Carmichael, promptly. But the worst paddock on Mulfera, in its worst season, was not more dry than the manager's tone.

Shortly before eleven the bell was rung which roused the men on week-day mornings, and they began trooping over from their hut, while the trio foregathered on the veranda as before. The open end was the one looking east but the sun was too near the zenith to enter many inches, and with equal thoroughness and tact Carmichael had placed the table, the water-bag, and the tumbler, at the open end. They were all that he could do in the way of pulpit, desk, and lectern.

The men tramped in and filled the chairs, forms, tin trunks, and packing-cases which had been pressed into the service of this makeshift sanctuary. The trio sat in front. The bell ceased, the ringer entering and taking his place. There was some delay, if not some hitch. Then came the chaplain with an anxious face.

'His lordship wishes to know if all hands are here,' he whispered across the desk.

Carmichael looked behind him for several seconds. 'Every man Jack,' he replied. 'And damn his lordship's cheek!' he added for his equals' benefit, as the chaplain disappeared.

'Rum cove, that chaplain,' whispered Chaucer, in the guarded manner of one whose frequent portion is the snub brutal.

'How so?' inquired Carmichael, with a duly withering glance.

Chaucer told in whispers of a word which he had overheard through the weatherboard wall of the room in which the Bishop had sought repose. It was, in fact, the monosyllable of which Carmichael had just made use. He, however, was the first to heap discredit on the book-keeper's story, which he laughed to scorn with as much of his usual arrogance as could be assumed below the breath.

'If you heard it at all,' said Carmichael, 'which I don't for a moment believe, you heard it in the strictly Biblical sense. You can't be expected to know what that is, Chaucer, but as a matter of fact it means lost and done for, like our noble selves. And it was probably applied to us, if there's the least truth in what you say.'

'Truth!' he began, but was not suffered to add another word.

'Shut up,' snarled Carmichael. 'Can't you hear them coming?'

And the tramp of the shooting-boots, which Dr. Methuen was still new chum enough to wear, followed by the chaplain's lighter step, drew noisily nearer upon the unseen part of the veranda that encircled the whole house.

'Stand up, you cripples!' cried Carmichael over his shoulder, in a stage whisper. And they all came to their feet as the two ecclesiastics appeared behind the table at the open end of the tabernacle.

Carmichael felt inclined to disperse the congregation on the spot.

There was the Bishop still in his gaiters and his yellow dust-coat; even the chaplain had not taken the trouble to don his surplice. So anything was good enough for Mulfera! Carmichael had lunged forward with a jutting jaw when an authoritative voice rang out across the table.

'Sit down!'

The Bishop had not opened his hairy mouth. It was the smart young chaplain who spoke. And all obeyed except Carmichael.

'I beg your lordship's pardon,' he was beginning, with sarcastic emphasis, when the manager of Mulfera was cut as short as he was himself in the habit of cutting his inferiors.

'If you will kindly sit down,' cried the chaplain, 'like everybody else, I shall at once explain the apparent irregularity upon which you were doubtless about to comment.'

Carmichael glowered through his glasses for a few seconds, and then resumed his seat with a shrug and a murmur, happily inaudible to all but his two immediate neighbors.

'On his way here this morning,' the chaplain went on, 'his lordship met with a misadventure from which he has not yet recovered sufficiently to address you as he fully hoped and intended to do to-day.' At this all eyes sped to the Bishop, who stood certainly in a drooping attitude at the chaplain's side, his episcopal hands behind his back. 'Something happened,' the glib spokesman continued with stern eyes, 'something that you do not often hear of in these days. His lordship was accosted, beset, and, like the poor man in the Scriptures, despitefully entreated, not many miles beyond your own boundary, by a pair of armed ruffians!'

'Stuck up!' cried one or two, and 'Bushrangers!' one or two more.

'I thank you for both words,' said the chaplain, bowing. 'He was stuck up by the bushranger who is once more abroad in the land. Really, Mr. Carmichael — '

But the manager of Mulfera rose to his full height, and, leaning back to get the speaker into focus, stuck his arms akimbo in a way that he had in his most aggressive moments.

'And what were *you* doing?' he demanded fiercely of the chaplain.

'It was I who stuck him up,' answered the *soi-disant* chaplain, whipping a single glass into his eye to meet the double ones. 'My name is Stingaree!'

And in the instant's hush which followed he plucked a revolver from his breast, while the hands of the sham bishop shot out from behind his back, with one in each.

The scene of the instant after that defies

ordinary description. It was made the more hideous by the frightful imprecations of Carmichael, and the short, sharp threat of Stingaree to shoot him dead unless he instantly sat down. Carmichael bade him do so with a gallant oath, at which the men immediately behind him joined with his two companions in pulling him back into his chair and there holding him by main force. Thereafter the manager appeared to realize the futility of resistance, and was unhanded on his undertaking to sit quiet, which he did with the exception of one speech to those behind.

'If any of you happen to be armed,' he shouted over his shoulder, 'shoot him down like a dog. But if you're all as fairly had as I am, let's hear what the beggar's got to say.'

'Thank you, Mr. Carmichael,' said the bushranger, still from the far side of the table, as a comparative silence fell at last. 'You are a man after my own heart, sir, and I would as lief have you on my side as the simple ruffian on my right. Not a bad bishop to look at,' continued Stingaree, with a jerk of the head toward his mate with the two revolvers. 'But if I had let him open his mouth! Now, if I'd had you, Mr. Carmichael — but I have my doubts about your vocabulary, too!'

The point appealed to all present, and

there was a laugh, in which, however, Carmichael did not join.

'I suppose you didn't come here simply to give us a funny entertainment,' said he. 'I happen to be the boss, or have been hitherto, and if you will condescend to tell me what you want I shall consider whether it is worth while to supply you or to be shot by you. I shall be sorry to meet my death at the hands of a thieving blackguard, but one can't pick and choose in that matter. Before it comes to choosing, however, is it any good asking what you've done with the real bishop and the real chaplain? If you've murdered them, as I — '

Stingaree had listened thus far with more than patience, in fact with something akin to approval, to the captive who was still his master with the tongue. With all his villainy, the bushranger was man enough to appreciate another man when he met him; but Carmichael's last word flicked him on a bare nerve.

'Don't you dare to talk to me about murder,' he rapped out. 'I've never committed one yet, but you're going the right way to make me begin! As for Bishop Methuen, I have more respect for him than for any man in Australia; but his horse was worth two of my mate's, and that's all I troubled him for. I didn't even tie him up as I would any other man. We just relieved the two of them of their boots and clothes, which was quite as good as tying up, with your roads as red-hot as they are — though my mate here doesn't agree with me.'

The man with the beard very emphatically shook a matted head, now relieved of the stolen helmet, and observed that the quicker they were the better it would be. He was as taciturn a bushranger as he had been a bishop, but Stingaree was perfectly right. Even these few words would have destroyed all chance of illusion in the case of his mate.

'The very clothes, which become us so well,' continued the prince of personators, who happened to be without hair upon his face at this period, and who looked every inch his part; 'their very boots, we have only borrowed! I will tell you presently where we dropped the rest of their kit. We left them a suit of pyjamas apiece, and not another stitch, and we blindfolded and drove 'em into the scrub as a last precaution. But before we go I shall also tell you where a search-party is likely to pick up their tracks. Meanwhile you will all stay exactly where you are, with the exception of the store-keeper, who will kindly accompany me to the store. I shall naturally require to see the inside of the safe, but otherwise our wants are very simple.'

The outlaw ceased. There was no word in answer; a curious hush had fallen on the captive congregation.

'If there is a store-keeper,' suggested Stingaree, 'he'd better stand up.'

But the accomplished Chaucer sat stark and staring.

'Up with you,' whispered Carmichael, in terrible tones, 'or we're done!'

And even as the book-keeper rose tremulously to his feet, and strange and stealthy figure, the cynosure of all eyes but the bushrangers' for a long minute, reached the open end of the veranda; and with a final spring, a tall man in silk pyjamas, his gray beard flying over either shoulder, hurled himself upon both bushrangers at once. With outspread fingers he clutched the scruff of each neck at the self-same second, crash came the two heads together, and over went the table with the three men over it.

Shots were fired in the struggle on the ground, happily without effect. Stingaree had his shooting hand mangled by one blow with a chair whirled from a height. Carmichael got his heel with a venomous stamp upon the neck of Howie; and, in fewer seconds than it would take to write their names, the rascals were defeated and disarmed. Howie had his neck half broken, and his face was darkening before Carmichael could be induced to lift his foot.

'The cockroach!' bawled the manager, drunk with battle. 'I'd hoof his soul out for two pins!'

A moment later he was groping for his glasses, which had slipped and fallen from his perspiring nose, and making use of such expressions withal as to compel a panting protest from the tall man in the silken stripes.

'My name is Methuen,' said he. 'I know it's a special moment, but — do you mind?'

Carmichael found his glasses at that instant, adjusted them, stood up, and leant back to view the Bishop; and his next words were the apology of the gentleman he should have been.

'My dear fellow,' cried the other, 'I quite understand. What are they doing with the ruffians? Have you any handcuffs? Is it far to the nearest police barracks?'

But the next act of this moving melodrama was not the least characteristic of the chief performance; for when Stingaree and partner had been not only handcuffed but lashed hand and foot, and incarcerated in separate log-huts, with a guard apiece; and when a mounted messenger had been despatched to the barracks at Clare Corner, and the remnant raised a cheer for Bishop Methuen;

it was then that the fine fellow showed them the still finer stuff of which he was also made. He invited all present to step back for a few minutes into the place of worship which had been so charmingly prepared, so scandalously misused, and where he hoped to see them all yet again in the evening, if it would not bore them to give him a further and more formal hearing then.

'I won't keep them five minutes now,' he whispered to Carmichael, as the men went ahead to pick up the chairs and take their places, while the Bishop hobbled after, still in his pyjamas, and with terribly inflamed and swollen feet. 'And then,' he added, 'I must ask you to send a buggy at once for my poor chaplain. He did his gallant best, poor fellow, but I had to leave him fallen by the way. I am an old miler, you know; it came easier to me; but the cinder-path and running-shoes are a different story from hot sand and naked feet! And now, if you please, I will strike one little blow while our hearts are still warm.'

But how shrewdly he struck it, how straight from the shoulder, how simply, how honestly, there is perhaps no need to tell even those who have no previous knowledge of back-block Bishop Methuen and his manly ways.

What afterward happened to Stingaree is another matter, to be set forth faithfully in the sequel. This is the story of the Purification of Mulfera Station, N.S.W., in which the bushrangers played but an indirect and a most inglorious part.

The Bishop and his chaplain (a good man of no present account) stayed to see the police arrive that night, and the romantic ruffians taken thence next morning in unromantic bonds. Comparatively little attention was paid to their departure — partly on account of the truculent attitude of the police — partly because the Episcopal pair were making an equally early start in another direction. No one accompanied the armed men and the bound. But every man on the place, from homestead, men's hut, rabbiter's tent, and boundary-rider's camp — every single man who could be mustered for the nonce had a horse run up for him — escorted Dr. Methuen in close cavalcade to the Mulfera boundary, where the final cheering took place, led by Carmichael, who, of course, was font and origin of the display. And Carmichael rode by himself on the way back; he had been much with the Bishop during his lordship's stay; and he was too morose for profanity during the remainder of that day.

But it was no better when the manager's

mood lifted, and the life on Mulfera slipped back into the old blinding and perspiring groove.

Then one night, a night of the very week thus sensationally begun, the ingenious Chaucer began one of the old, old stories, on the moonlit veranda, and Carmichael stopped him while that particular old story was still quite young in the telling. There was an awkward pause until Carmichael laughed.

'I don't care twopence what you fellows think of me,' said he, 'and never did. I saw a lot of the Bishop,' he went on, less aggressively, after a pause.

'So *we* saw,' assented Smart.

'You bet!' added Chaucer.

For they were two to one.

'He ran the mile for Oxford,' continued Carmichael. 'Two years he ran it — and won both times. You may not appreciate quite what that means.'

And, with a patience foreign to his character as they knew it, Carmichael proceeded to explain.

'But,' he added, 'that was nothing to his performance last Sunday, in getting here from beyond the boundary in the time he did it in — barefoot! It would have been good enough in shoes. But don't you forget his feet. I can see them — and feel them — still.'

'Oh, he's a grand chap,' the overseer allowed.

'We never said he wasn't,' his ally chimed in.

Carmichael took no notice of a tone which the youth with the putty face had never employed toward him before.

'He was also in his school eleven,' continued Carmichael, still in a reflective fashion.

'Was it a public school?' inquired Smart.

'Yes.'

'*The* public school?' added Chaucer.

'Not mine, if that's what you mean,' returned Carmichael, with just a touch of his earlier manner. 'But — he knew my old Head Master — he was quite a pal of the dear Old Man! ... We had such lots in common,' added the manager, more to himself than to the other two.

The overseer's comment is of no consequence. What the book-keeper was emboldened to add matters even less. Suffice it that between them they brought the old Carmichael to his feet, his glasses flaming in the moonshine, his body thrown pugilistically backward, his jaw jutting like a crag — the old Carmichael in deed — but not in word.

'I told you just now I didn't care twopence what either of you thought of me,' he roared, 'though there wasn't the least necessity to tell you, because you knew! So I needn't repeat myself; but just listen a moment, and try not to be greater fools than God made you. You saw a real man last Sunday, and so did I. I had almost forgotten what they were like — that quality. Well, we had a lot of talk, and he told me what they are doing on some of the other stations. They are holding services, something like what he held here, every Sunday night for themselves. Now, it isn't in human nature to fly from one extreme to the other: but we are going to have a try to keep up our Sunday end with the other stations; at least I am, and you two are going to back me up.'

He paused. Not a syllable from the pair.

'Do you hear me?' thundered Carmichael, as he had thundered in the dormitory at school, now after twenty years in the same good cause once more. 'Whether you like it or not, you fellows are going to back me up!'

And Carmichael was a mighty man, whose influence was not to be withstood.

A Duel in the Desert

It was eight o'clock and Monday morning when the romantic rascals were led away in unromantic bonds. Their arms were bound to their bodies, their feet lashed to the stirrup-irons; they sat like packs upon quiet station horses, carefully chosen for the nonce; they were tethered to a mounted policeman apiece, each with leading-rein buckled to his left wrist and Government revolver in his right hand. Behind the quartette rode the officer in command, superbly mounted, watching ever all four with a third revolver ready cocked. It seemed a small and yet an ample escort for the two bound men.

But Stingaree was by no means in that state of Napoleonic despair which his bent back and lowering countenance were intended to convey. He had not uttered a word since the arrival of the police, whom he had suffered to lift him on horseback, as he now sat, without raising his morose eyes once. Howie, on the other hand, had offered a good deal of futile opposition, cursing his captors as the fit moved him, and once struggling so insanely in his bonds as to earn a tap from the wrong

185

end of a revolver and a bloody face for his pains. Stingaree glowered in deep delight. His mate's part was as well acted as his own; but it was he who had conceived them both, and expounded them in countless camps against some such extremity as this. The result was in ideal accordance with his calculations. The man who gave the trouble was the man to watch. And Stingaree, chin on chest, was left in peace to evolve a way of escape.

The chances were all adverse; he had never been less sanguine in his life. Not that Stingaree had much opinion of the police; he had slipped through their hands too often; but it was an unfortunate circumstance that two of the present trio were among those whom he had eluded most recently, and who therefore would be least likely to give him another chance. A lightning student of his kind, he based his only hope upon an accurate estimate of these men, and applied his whole mind to the triple task. But it was a single task almost from the first; for the policeman in charge of him was none other than his credulous old friend, Sergeant Cameron from Clear Corner; and Howie's custodian, a young trooper run from the same mould as Constable Tyler and many a hundred more, in whom a thick skull cancelled a stout heart. Both were brave men;

neither was really to be feared. But the man behind upon the thoroughbred, the man in front, the man now on this side and now on that, with his braying laugh and his vindictive voice — triumphant as though he had taken the bushrangers himself, and a blatant bully in his triumph — was none other than the formidable Superintendent whose undying animosity the bushrangers had earned by the two escapades associated with his name.

Yet the outlaw never flattered him with word or look, never lifted chin from chest, never raised an eye or opened his mouth until Howie's knock on the head caused him to curse his mate for a fool who deserved all he got. The thoroughbred was caracoling on his other side in an instant.

'You ain't one, are you?' cried the taunting tongue of Superintendent Cairns. 'Not much fool about Stingaree!'

The time had come for a reply.

'So I thought until yesterday,' sighed the bushranger. 'But now I'm not so sure.'

'Not so sure, eh? You were sure enough last time we met, my beauty!'

'Yes! I had some conceit of myself then,' said Stingaree, with another of his convincing sighs.

'To say nothing of when you guyed me,

damn you!' added the Superintendent, below his breath and through his teeth.

'Well,' replied the outlaw, 'you've got your revenge. I must expect you to rub it in.'

'My fine friend,' rejoined Cairns, 'you may expect worse than that, and still you won't be disappointed.'

Stingaree made no reply; and it would have taken a very shrewd eye to have read deeper than the depth of sullen despair expressed in every inch of his bound body and every furrow of his downcast face. Even the vindictive Cairns ceased for a time to crow over so abject an adversary in so bitter an hour. Meanwhile, the five horses streamed slowly through the high lights and heavy shadows of a winding avenue of scrub. It was like a hot-house in the dense, low trees: not a wandering wind, not a waking bird; but five faces that dripped steadily in the shade, and all but caught fire in the sun. Ahead rode Howie, dazed and bleeding, with his callous young constable; the sergeant and his chief, with Stingaree between them, now brought up the rear. By degrees Stingaree raised his chin a little, but still looked neither right nor left.

'Cheer up!' cried the chief, with soothing irony.

'I feel the heat,' said the bound man,

uncomplainingly. 'And it was just about here it happened.'

'What happened?'

'We overtook the Church militant here on earth,' rejoined the bushranger, with rueful irreverence.

'Well, you ran against a snag that time, Mr. Sanguinary Stingaree!'

'I couldn't resist turning Howie into the Bishop and making myself his mouthpiece. I daren't let him open his lips! It wasn't the offertory that was worth having; it was the fun of rounding up that congregation on the homestead veranda, and never letting them spot a thing till we'd showed our guns. There hadn't been a hitch, and never would have been if that old Bishop hadn't run all those miles barefoot over hot sand and taken us unawares.'

Made with wry humor and a philosophic candor, alike germane to his predicament, these remarks seemed natural enough to one knowing little of Stingaree. They seemed just the sort of things that Stingaree would say. The effect, however, was rather to glorify Bishop Methuen at the expense of Superintendent Cairns, who strove to reverse it with some dexterity.

'You certainly ran against a snag,' he repeated, 'and now your mate's run against another.' He gave the butt of his ready pistol a significant tap. 'But I'm the worst snag that ever either of you struck,' he went on in his vainglory. 'Make no mistake about that. And the worst day's work that ever you did in your life, Mr. Sanguinary Stingaree, was when you dared to play at being little crooked Cairns.'

Stingaree took a first good look at his man. After all he was not so crooked on horseback as he had seemed on foot at dusk in the Victorian bush; his hump was even less pronounced than Stingaree himself had made it on Rosanna; it looked more like a ridge of extra muscle across a pair of abnormally broad and powerful shoulders. There was the absence of neck which this deformity suggests; there was a great head lighted by flashing and indignant eyes, but mounted only on its mighty chin. The bushranger was conceited enough to find in the flesh a coarser and more common type than that created by himself for the honor of the road. But this did not make the real Superintendent a less formidable foe.

'The most poetic justice!' murmured Stingaree, and resumed in an instant his apathetic pose.

'It serves you jolly well right, if that's what you mean,' the Superintendent snarled.

'You've yourself and your own mighty cheek to thank for taking me out of my shell and putting me on your tracks in earnest. But it was high time they knew the cut of my jib up here; the fools won't forget me again in a hurry. And you, you devil, you sha'n't forget me till your dying day!'

On Stingaree's off-side Sergeant Cameron was also hanging an insulted head. But the bushranger laughed softly in his chest.

'Someone has got to do your dirty work,' said he. 'I did it that time, and the Bishop has done it now; but you shouldn't blame me for helping your fellows to bring a murderer to justice.'

'You guyed me,' said Cairns through his teeth. 'I heard all about it. You guyed me, blight your soul!'

Stingaree felt that he was missing a strong face finely convulsed with passion — as indeed he was. But he had already committed the indiscretion of a repartee, which was scarcely consistent with an attitude of extreme despair. A downcast silence seemed the safest policy after all.

'It used to be forty miles to the Corner,' he murmured, after a time. 'We can't have come more than ten.'

'Not so much,' snapped the Superintendent.

'Going to stop for feed at Mazeppa Station?'

'That's my business.'

'It's a long day for three of you, in this heat, with two of us.'

'The time won't hang heavy on *our* hands.'

'Not heavy enough, I should have thought. I wonder you didn't bring some of the boys from Mulfera along with you.'

Superintendent Cairns brayed his high, harsh laugh.

'Yes, you wonder, and so did they,' said he. 'But I know a bit too much. There'll always be sympathy among scum like them for thicker scum like you!'

'You're too suspicious,' said Stingaree, mildly. 'But I was thinking of the Bishop and the boss.'

'They've gone their own way,' growled Cairns, 'and it's just as well it wasn't our way. I'd have stood no interference from them!'

That had been his attitude on the station. Stingaree had heard of his rudeness to those to whom the whole credit of the capture belonged; the man revealed his character as freely as an angry child; and, indeed, a childish character it was. Arrogance was its strength and weakness: a suggestion had only to be made to call down either the insolence

192

of office or the malice of denial for denial's sake.

'I wish you'd stop a bit at Mazeppa,' whined Stingaree, drooping like a candle in the heat.

The station roofs gleamed through the trees far off the track.

'Why?'

'Because I'm feeling sick.'

'Gammon! You've got some friends there; on you push!'

'But you will camp somewhere in the heat of the day?'

'I'll do as I think fit. I sha'n't consult you, my fine friend.'

Stingaree drooped and nodded, lower and lower; then recovered himself with a jerk, like one battling against sleep. The party pushed on for another hour. The heat was terrible; the bound men endured torments in their bonds. But the nature of the Superintendent, deformed like his body, declared itself duly at every turn, and the more one prisoner groaned and the other blasphemed, the greater the zest and obduracy of the driving force behind them.

Noon passed; the scanty shadows length-ened; and Howie gave more trouble of an insensate sort. They reined up, and lashed him tighter; he had actually loosened his cords. But Stingaree seemed past remonstrance with friend or foe, and his bound body swayed from side to side as the little cavalcade went on at a canter to make up for lost time.

He was leading now with the kindly sergeant, and his mind had never been more alert. Behind them thundered the recalcitrant Howie with constable and Superintendent on either side. They were midway between Mazeppa and Clear Corner, or some fifteen miles from either haunt of men. Stingaree pulled himself upright in the saddle as by a superhuman effort, and shook off the helping hand that held him by one elbow.

He was about to do a thing at which even his courage quailed, and he longed for the use of his right arm. It was not absolutely bound; the hand and wrist had been badly hurt in the Sunday's fray — so badly that it had been easy to sham a fracture, and have hand and wrist in splints before the arrival of the police. They still hung before him in a sling, his good right hand and fore-arm, stiff and sore enough, yet strong and ready at a moment's notice, when the moment came. It had not come, and was not coming for a long time, when Stingaree set his teeth, lurched either way — and toppled out of the saddle in the path of the cantering hoofs. His lashed feet held him in the stirrups; the off stirrup-leather had come over with his weight; and there at his horse's hoofs, kicked and trampled and smothered with blood and dust, he dragged like an anchor, without sign of life.

And it was worse even than it looked, for the life never left him for an instant, nor ever for an instant did he fail to behave as though it had. Minutes later, when they had stopped his horse, and cut him down from the stirrups, and carried him into the shade of a hop-bush off the track, and when Stingaree dared to open his eyes, he was nearer closing them perforce, and the scene swam before him with superfluous realism.

Cairns and Cameron, dismounted (while the trooper sat aloof with Howie in the saddle), were at high words about their prostrate prisoner. Not a syllable was lost on Stingaree.

'You may put him across the horse yourself,' said the sergeant. 'I won't have a hand in it. But make sure you haven't killed him as it is — travelling a sick man like that.'

'Killed him? He's got his eyes open!' cried Cairns in savage triumph. Stingaree lay blinking at the sky. 'Do you still refuse to do your duty?'

'Cruelty to animals is no duty of mine,'

declared the sergeant: 'let alone my fellow-men, bushrangers or no bushrangers.'

'And you?' thundered Cairns at the mounted constable.

'I'm with the sergeant,' said he. 'He's had enough.'

'Right!' cried the Superintendent, producing a note-book and scribbling venomously. 'You both refuse! You will hear more of this; meanwhile, sergeant, I should like to know what your superior wisdom may be pleased to suggest.'

'Send a cart back for him,' said Cameron. 'It's the only way he's fit to travel.'

Stingaree sought to prop himself upon the elbow of the splintered wrist and hand.

'There are no more bones broken that I know of,' said he, faintly. 'But I felt bad before, and now I feel worse.'

'He looks it, too,' observed the sergeant, as Stingaree, ghastly enough beneath his blood and dust, rolled over on his back once more, and lay effectively with closed eyes. Even the Superintendent was impressed.

'Then what's to be done with him?' he exclaimed, with an oath. 'What's to be done?'

'If you ask me,' returned Cameron, 'I should make him comfortable where he is; after all, he's a human being, and done no murder, that we should run the risk of murdering him. Leave him to me while you two push on with his mate; then one of you can get back with the spring-cart before sundown; but trust me to look after him till you do.'

Stingaree held his breath where he lay. His excitement was not to be betrayed by the opening of an eye. And yet he knew that the Superintendent was looking the sergeant up and down, and he guessed what was passing through that suspicious mind.

'Trust you!' rasped the dictatorial voice at last. 'That's the very thing I'm not inclined to do, Sergeant Cameron.'

'Sir!'

'Keep your temper, sergeant. I don't say you'd let him go. But I've got to remember that this man has twisted you round his finger before to-day, led you by the hand like a blessed old child, and passed himself off for me! Look at the fellow; look at me; and ask yourself candidly if you're the man for the job. But don't ask me, unless you want my opinion of you a bit plainer still. No; you go on with the others. The two of you can manage Howie; if you can't, you put a bullet through him! This is my man; and I'm his, by the hokey, as he'll know if he tries any of his tricks while you're gone!'

Stingaree did not move a muscle. He might

have been dead; and in his disappointment it was the easier to lie as though he were. Really bruised, really battered, really faint and stiff and sore, to say nothing of his bonds, he felt himself physically no match for so young a man — with the extra breadth of shoulder and the extra length of arm which were part and parcel of his deformity. With the elderly sergeant he might have had a chance, man to man, one arm to two; but with Superintendent Cairns his only weapons were his wits. He lay quite still and reviewed the situation, as it was, and as it had been. In the very moment of his downfall, by instinctive presence of mind he had preserved the use of his right hand, and that was a still unsuspected asset of incalculable worth. It had been the nucleus of all his plans; without a hand he must have resigned himself to the inevitable from the first. Then he had split up the party. He heard the sergeant and the constable ride off with Howie, exactly as he had intended two of the three captors to do. His fall alone introduced the element of luck. It might have killed or maimed him; but the risk had been run with open eyes. Being alive and whole, he had reduced the odds from three against two to man and man; and the difference was enormous, even though one man held all the cards. Against Howie the odds were heavier than ever, but Howie was eliminated from present calculations. And as Stingaree made them with the upturned face of seeming insensibility, he heard a nonchalant step come and go, but knew an eye was on him all the time, and never opened his own till the striking of a match was followed by the smell of bush tobacco.

The shadow of the hop-bush was spreading like spilt ink, and for the moment Stingaree thought he had it to himself. But a wreath of blue smoke hovered overhead; and when he got to his elbow, and glanced behind, there sat Cairns in his shirt-sleeves, filling the niche his body made in the actual green bush, a swollen wet water-bag at his feet, his revolver across his knees. There was an ominous click even as Stingaree screwed round where he lay.

'Give me a drink!' he cried at sight of the humid canvas bag.

'Why should I?' asked the Superintendent, smoking on.

'Because I haven't had one since we started — because I'm parched with thirst.'

'Parch away!' cried the creature of suspicion. 'You can't help yourself, and I can't help you with this baby to nurse.'

And he fondled the cocked revolver in his hands.

'Very well! Don't give me one!' exclaimed Stingaree, and dealt the moist bag a kick that sent a jet of cold water spurting over his foot. He expected to be kicked himself for that; he was only cursed, the bag snatched out of his reach, and deeply drained before his eyes.

'I was going to give you some,' said Cairns, smacking his lips. 'Now your tongue may hang out before I do.'

Stingaree left the last word with the foe: it was part of his preconceived policy. He still regretted his solitary retort, but not for a moment the more petulant act which he had just committed. His boots had been removed after his fall; one of his socks was now wet through, and he spent the next few minutes in taking it off with the other foot. The lengthy process seemed to afford his mind a certain pensive entertainment. It was a shapely and delicate white foot that lay stripped at last — a foot that its owner, with nothing better to do, could contemplate with legitimate satisfaction. But Superintendent Cairns, noting his prisoner's every look, and putting his own confident interpretation on them all, cursed him afresh for a conceited pig, and filled another pipe, with the revolver for an instant by his side.

Stingaree took no interest in his proceedings; the revolver he especially ignored, and lay stretched before his captor, one sock off and one sock on, one arm in splints and sling and the other bound to his ribs, a model prisoner whose last thought was of escape. His legs, indeed, were free; but a man who could not sit on a horse was not the man to run away. And then there was the relentless Superintendent sitting over him, pipe in mouth, but revolver again in hand, and a crooked finger very near the trigger.

The fiery wilderness still lay breathless in the great heat, but the lengthening shadow of the hop-bush was now a thing to be thankful for, and in it the broken captive fell into a fine semblance of natural slumber. Cairns watched with alternate envy and suspicion; for him there could not be a wink; but most likely the fellow was shamming all the time. No ruse, however, succeeded in exposing the sham, which the Superintendent copied by breathing first heavily and then stertorously, with one eye open and on his man. Stingaree never opened one of his: there was no change in the regular breathing, in the peaceful expression of the blood-stained face: asleep the man must be. The Superintendent's own experiments had gone to show him that no extremity need necessarily keep one awake in such heat. He stifled a yawn that was no part of his performance. His pipe was out; he struck a match noisily on his boot; and Stingaree just stirred, as naturally as any infant. But Stingaree's senses were incredibly acute. He smelt every whiff of the rekindled pipe, knew to ten seconds when it went out once more, and listened in an agony for another match. None was struck. Was the Superintendent himself really asleep this time? He breathed as though he were; but so did Stingaree; and yet was there hope in the fact that his own greatest struggle all this time had been against the very thing he feigned.

At last he opened one eye a little; it was met by no answering furtive glance; he opened the other, and there could be no more doubt. The terrible Superintendent was dozing in his place; but it was the lightest sort of doze, the eyes were scarcely closed, and all but watching Stingaree, as the cocked revolver in the relaxed hand all but covered him.

The prisoner felt that for the moment he was unseen, forgotten, but that the lightest movement of his body would open those terrible eyes once and for all. Be it remembered that he was lying under them lengthwise, on the bound arm, with the arm in the sling uppermost, and easily to be freed, but yet the most salient part of the recumbent figure, and that on which the hidden eyes still seemed fixed, for all their lids. To make the least movement there, to attempt the slowest withdrawal of hand and arm, was to court the last disaster of discovery in such an act. But to lie motionless down to the thighs, and to execute a flank movement with the leg uppermost, was a far less perilous exploit. It was the leg with the bare foot: every detail had been foreseen. And now at last the bare foot hovered over the revolver and the hand it held, while the upper man yet lay like a log under those drowsy, dreadful eyes.

Stingaree took a last look at the barrel drooping from the slackened hand; the back of the hand lay on the ground, the muzzle of the barrel was filled with sand, and yet the angle was such that it was by no means sure whether a bullet would bury itself in the sand or in Stingaree. He took the risk, and with his bare toe he touched the trigger sharply. There was a horrible explosion. It brought the drowsy Superintendent to his senses with such a jerk that it was as though the smoking pistol had leapt out of his hand a thing alive, and so into the hand that flashed to meet it from the sling. And almost in the same second — while the double cloud of smoke and sand still hung between them — Stingaree sprang from the ground, an armed man once more.

'Sit where you are!' he thundered. 'Up with those hands before I shoot them to shreds! Your life's in less danger than mine has been all day, but I'll wing you limb by limb if you offer to budge!'

With uplifted hands above his ears, the deformed officer sat with head and shoulders depressed into the semblance of one sphere. Not a syllable did he utter; but his upturned eyes shot indomitable fires. Stingaree stood wriggling and fumbling at the coil which bound his left arm to his side; suddenly the revolver went off, as if by accident, but so much by design that there dangled two ends of rope, cut and burnt asunder by lead and powder. In less than a minute the bushranger was unbound, and before the minute was up he had leapt upon the Superintendent's thoroughbred. It had been tethered all this time to a tree, swishing tails with the station hack which Stingaree had ridden as a captive; he now rode the thoroughbred, and led the hack, to the very feet of the humiliated Cairns.

'I will thank you for that water-bag,' said Stingaree. 'I am much obliged. And now I'll trouble you for that nice wideawake. You really don't need it in the shade. Thank you so much!'

He received both bag and hat on the barrel

of the Government revolver, hooking the one to its proper saddle-strap, and clapping on the other at an angle inimitably imitative of the outwitted officer.

'I won't carry the rehearsal any further to your face,' continued Stingaree; 'but I can at least promise you a more flattering portrait than the last; and this excellent coat, which you have so considerately left strapped to your saddle, should contribute greatly to the verisimilitude. Dare I hope that you begin to appreciate some of the points of my performance so far as it has gone? The pretext on which I bared my foot for its delicate job under your very eyes, eh? Not so vain as it looked, in either sense, I fancy! Should you have said that your hand would recoil from a revolver the moment it went off? You see, I staked my life on it, and I've won. And what about that fall? It was the lottery! I was prepared to have my head cracked like an egg, and it's still pretty sore. The broken wrist wasn't your fault; it had passed into the accepted situation before you turned up. And you would certainly have seen that I was shamming sleep if we hadn't both been so genuinely sleepy at the time. I give you my word, I very nearly threw up the whole thing for forty winks! Any other point on which you could wish enlightenment? Then let me thank you with all my heart for one of the worst days, and some of the greatest moments, in my whole career.'

But the crooked man answered never a word, as he sat in a ball with uplifted palms, and glaring, upturned, unconquerable eyes.

'Good-by, Mr. Superintendent Cairns,' said Stingaree. 'I'm afraid I've been rather cruel to you — but you were never very nice to me!'

Sergeant Cameron was driving the spring-cart, toward sundown, after a variety of unforeseen delays. Of a sudden out of the pink haze came a galloping figure, slightly humped, in the inspector's coat and wide-awake, with a bare foot through one stirrup and only a sock on its fellow.

'Where's Stingaree?' screamed the sergeant, pulling up. And the galloper drew rein at the driven horse's head.

'Dead!' said he, thickly. 'He was worse than we thought. You fetch him while I — '

But this time the sergeant knew that voice too well, and his right hand had flown to the back of his belt. Stingaree's shot was only first by a fraction of a second, but it put a bullet through the brain of the horse between the shafts, so that horse and shafts came down together, and the sergeant fired into the earth as he fell across the splashboard.

Stingaree pressed soft heels into the thoroughbred's ribs and thundered on and on. Soon there was a gate to open, and when he listened at that gate all was still behind him and before; but far ahead the rolling plain was faintly luminous in the dusk, and as this deepened into night a cluster of terrestrial lights sprang out with the stars. Stingaree knew the handful of gaunt, unsheltered huts the lights stood for. They were an inn, a store, and police-barracks: Clear Corner on the map. The bushranger galloped straight up to the barracks, but skirted the knot of men in the light before the veranda, and went jingling round into the yard. The young constable in charge ran through the building and met him dismounted at the back.

'What's the matter, sir?'

'He's gone!'

'Stingaree?'

'He was worse than we thought. Your man all right?'

'No trouble whatever, sir. Only sick and sorry and saying his prayers in a way you'd never credit. Come and hear him.'

'I must come and see him at once. Got a fresh horse in?'

'I have so! In and saddled in the stall. I thought you might want one, sir, and ran up

Barmaid, Stingaree's own mare, that was sent out here from the station when we had the news.'

'That was very thoughtful of you. You'll get on, young man. Now lead the way with that lamp.'

This time Stingaree had spoken in gasps, like a man who had ridden very far, and the young constable, unlike his sergeant, did not know his voice of old. Yet it struck him at the last moment as more unlike the voice of Superintendent Cairns than the hardest riding should have made it, and with the key in the door of the cell the young fellow wheeled round and held the lamp on high. That instant he was felled to the floor, the lamp went down and out with a separate yet simultaneous crash, and Stingaree turned the key.

'Howie! Not a word — out you come!'

The burly ruffian crept forth with outstretched hands apart.

'What! Not even handcuffed?'

'No; turned over a new leaf the moment we left you, and been praying like a parson for 'em all to hear!'

'This chap can do the same when he comes to himself. Lies pretty still, doesn't he? In with him!'

The door clanged. The key was turned.

208

Stingaree popped it into his pocket.

'The later they let him out the better. Here's the best mount you ever had. And my sweetheart's waiting for me in the stable!'

Outside, in front, before the barracks veranda, an inquisitive little group heard first the clang of the door within, and presently the clatter of hoofs coming round from the yard. Stingaree and Howie — a white flash and a bay streak — swept past them as they stood confounded. And the dwindling pair still bobbed in sight, under a full complement of stars, when a fresh outcry from the cell, and a mighty hammering against its locked door, broke the truth to one and all.

The Villain-Worshipper

There was no more fervent admirer of Stingaree and all bushrangers than George Oswald Abernethy Melvin. Despite this mellifluous nomenclature young Melvin helped his mother to sell dance-music, ballads, melodeons, and a very occasional pianoforte, in one of the several self-styled capitals of Riverina; and despite both facts the mother was a lady of most gentle blood. The son could either teach or tune the piano with a certain crude and idle skill. He endured a monopoly of what little business the locality provided in this line, and sat superior on the music-stool at all the dances. He had once sung tenor in Bishop Methuen's choir, but, offended by a word of wise and kindly advice, was seen no more in surplice or in church. It will be perceived that Oswald Melvin had all the aggressive independence of Young Australia without the virility which leavens the truer type.

Yet he was neither a base nor an unkind lad. His bane was a morbid temperament, which he could no more help than his sallow face and weedy person; even his vanity was directly traceable to the early influence of an eccentric and feckless father with experimental ideas on the upbringing of a child. It was a pity that brilliantly unsuccessful man had not lived to see the result of his sedulous empiricism. His wife was left to bear the brunt — a brave exile whose romantic history was never likely to escape her continent lips. None even knew whether she saw any or one of those aggravated faults of an only child which were so apparent to all her world.

And yet the worst of Oswald Melvin was known only to his own morbid and sensitive heart. An unimpressive presence in real life, on his mind's stage he was ever in the limelight with a good line on his lips. Not that he was invariably the hero of these pieces. He could see himself as large with the noose round his neck as in coronet or halo; and though this inward and spiritual temper may be far from rare, there had been no one to kick out of him its outward and visible expression. Oswald had never learned to gulp down the little lie which insures a flattering attention; his clever father had even encouraged it in him as the nucleus of imagination. Imagination he certainly had, but it fed on strong meat for an unhealthy mind; it fattened on the sordid history of the earlier bushrangers; its favorite fare was the character and exploits of Stingaree. The sallow and neurotic face would brighten with morbid enthusiasm at the bare mention of the desperado's name. The somewhat dull, dark eyes would lighten with borrowed fires: the young fool wore an eye-glass in one of them when he dared.

'Stingaree,' he would say, 'is the greatest man in all Australia.' He had inherited from his father a delight in uttering startling opinions; but this one he held with unusual sincerity. It had come to all ears, and was the subject of that episcopal compliment which Oswald took as an affront. The impudent little choristers supported his loss by calling 'Stingaree!' after him in the street: he was wise to keep his eye-glass for the house.

There, however, with a few even younger men who admired his standpoint and revelled in his store of criminous annals, or with his patient, inscrutable mother, Oswald Melvin was another being. His language became bright and picturesque, his animation surprising. A casual customer would sometimes see this side of him, and carry away the impression of a rare young dare-devil. And it was one such who gave Oswald the first great moment of his bush life.

'Not been down from the back-blocks for three years?' he had asked, as he showed a tremulous and dilapidated bushman how to play the instrument that he had bought with the few shillings remaining out of his check. 'Been on the spree and going back to drive a whim until you've enough to go on another? How I wish you'd tell that to our high and mighty Lord Bishop of all the Back-Blocks! I should like to see his face and hear him on the subject; but I suppose he's new since you were down here last? Never come across him, eh? But, of course, you heard how good old Stingaree scored off him the other day, after he thought he'd scored off Stingaree?'

The whim-driver had heard something about it. Young Melvin plunged into the congenial narrative and emerged minutes later in a dusky glow.

★   ★   ★

'That's the man for my money,' he perorated. 'Stingaree, sir, is the greatest chap in all these Colonies, and deserves to be Viceroy when they get Federation. Thunderbolt, Morgan, Ben Hall and Ned Kelly were not a circumstance between them to Stingaree; and the silly old Bishop's a silly old fool to him! I don't care twopence about right and wrong. That's not the point. The one's a Force, and the other isn't.'

'A darned sight too much force, to my mind,' observed the whim-driver with some warmth.

'You don't take my meaning,' the superior youth pursued. 'It's a question of personality.'

'A bit more personal than you think,' was the dark rejoinder.

'How do you mean?'

Melvin's tone had altered in an instant.

'I know too much about him.'

'At first hand?' the youth asked, with bated breath.

'Double first!' returned the other, with a muddled glimmer of better things.

'You never knew him, did you?' whispered Oswald.

'Knew him? I've been taken prisoner by him,' said the whim-driver, with the pause of a man who hesitates to humiliate himself, but is lost for the sake of that same sensation which Oswald Melvin loved to create.

Mrs. Melvin was in the back room, wistfully engrossed in an English magazine sent that evening from Bishop's Lodge. The bad blood in the son had not affected Dr. Methuen's keen but tactful interest in the mother. She looked up in tolerant consternation as her Oswald pushed an unsavory bushman before him into the room; but even through her gentle horror the mother's love shone with that steady humor which raised it above the sphere of obvious pathos.

'Here's a man who's been stuck up by Stingaree!' he cried, boyish enough in his delight. 'Do keep an eye on the show, mother, and let him tell me all about it, as he's good enough to say he will. Is there any whiskey?'

'Not for me!' put in the whim-driver, with a frank shudder. 'I should like a drink of tea out of a cup, if I'm to have anything.'

Mrs. Melvin left them with a good-humored word besides her promise. She had given no sign of injury or disapproval; she was not one of the wincing sort; and the tremulous tramp was in her own chair before her back was turned.

'Now fire away!' cried the impatient Oswald.

'It's a long story,' said the whim-driver; and his dirty brows were knit in thought.

'Let's have it,' coaxed the young man. And the other's thoughtful creases vanished suddenly in the end.

'Very well,' said he, 'since it means a drink of tea out of a cup! It was only the other day, in a dust-storm away back near the Darling, as bad a one as ever I was out in. I was bushed and done for, gave it up and said my prayers. Then I practically died in my tracks, and came to life in a sunny clearing later in the day. The storm was over; two coves had found me and carried me to their camp; and as soon as I saw them I spotted one for Howie and the other for Stingaree!'

The narrative went no farther for a time. The thrilling youth fired question and leading question like a cross-examining counsel in a fever to conclude his case. The tea arrived, but the whim-driver had to help himself. His host neglected everything but the first chance he had ever had of hearing of Stingaree or any other bushranger at first-hand.

'And how long were you there?'

'About a week.'

'What happened then?'

The whim-driver paused in doubt renewed.

'You will never guess.'

'Tell me.'

'They waited for the next dust-storm, and then cast me adrift in that.'

Oswald stared; he would never have guessed, indeed. The unhealthy light faded from his sallow face. Even his morbid enthusiasm was a little damped.

'You must have done something to deserve it,' he cried, at last.

'I did,' was the reply, with hanging head. 'I — I tried to take him.'

'Take your benefactor — take him prisoner?'

'Yes — the man who saved my life.'

Melvin sat staring: it was a stare of honestly incredulous disgust. Then he sprang to his feet, a brighter youth than ever, his depression melted like a cloud. His villainous hero was an heroic villain after all! His heart of hearts — which was not black — could still render whole homage to Stingaree! He no longer frowned on his informer as on a thing accursed. The creature had wiped out his original treachery to Stingaree by replacing the uninjured idol in its niche in this warped mind. Oswald, however, had made his repugnance only too plain; he was unable to elicit another detail; and in a very few minutes Mrs. Melvin was back in her place, though not before flicking it with her handkerchief, undetected by her son.

It was certainly a battered and hang-dog figure that stole away into the bush. Yet the creature straightened as he strode into star-light undefiled by earthly illumination; his palsy left him; presently as he went he began fingering the new melodeon in the way of a man who need not have sought elementary instruction from Oswald Melvin. And now a shining disk filled one unwashed eye.

Stingaree lay a part of that night beside the milk-white mare that he had left tethered in a box-clump quite near the town; at sunrise he knelt and shaved on the margin of a Government tank, before breaking the mirror by plunging in. And before the next stars paled he was snugly back in older haunts, none knowing of his descent upon those of men.

There or thereabouts, hidden like the needle in the hay, and yet ubiquitous in the stack, the bushranger remained for months. Then there was an encounter, not the first of this period, but the first in which shots were exchanged. One of these pierced the lungs of his melodeon — an instrument more notorious by this time than the musical-box before it — a still greater treasure to Stingaree. That was near the full of a certain summer moon; it was barely waning to the eye when the battered buyer of melodeons came for a new one to the shop in the pretty bush town.

The shop was closed for the night, but Stingaree knocked at a lighted window under the veranda, which Mrs. Melvin presently threw up. Her eyes flashed when she recognized one against whom she now harbored a bitterness on quite a different plane of feeling from her former repulsion.

218

Even to his first glance she looked an older and a harder woman.

'I am sorry to see you,' she said, with a soft vehemence plainly foreign to herself. 'I almost hate the sight of you! You have been the ruin of my son!'

'His ruin?'

Stingaree forgot the speech of the unlettered stockman; but his cry was too short to do worse than warn him.

'Come round,' continued Mrs. Melvin, austerely. 'I will see you. You shall hear what you have done.'

In another minute he was in the parlor where he had sat aforetime. He never dreamt of sitting now. But the lady took her accustomed chair as a queen her throne.

'*Is* he ruined?' asked Stingaree.

'Not irrevocably — not yet; but he may be any moment. He must be before long.'

'But — but what ails him, madame?'

'Villain-worship!' cried the lady, with a tragic face stripped of all its humor, and bare without it as a winter's tree.

'I remember! Yes — I understand. He was mad about — Stingaree.'

'It is madness now,' said the bitter mother. 'It was only a stupid, hare-brained fancy then, but now it is something worse. You're the first to whom I have admitted it,' she continued, with illogical indignation, 'because it's all through you!'

'All through me?'

'You told him a tale. You made that villain a greater hero in his eyes than ever. You made him real.'

'He is real enough, God knows!'

'But you made him so to my son.' The keen eyes softened for one divine instant before they filled. 'And I — I am talking my own boy over with — with — '

Stingaree stood in twofold embarrassment. Did she know after all who he was? And what had he said he was, the time before?

'The lowest of the low,' he answered, with a twitch of his unshaven lips.

'No! That you were not, or are not, whatever you may say. You — ' she hesitated sweetly — 'you had been unsteady when you were here before.' He twitched again, imperceptibly. 'I am thankful to see that you are now more like what you must once have been. I can bear to tell you of my boy. Oh, sir, can you bear with me?'

Stingaree twitched no more. Rich as the situation was, keenly as he had savored its unsuspected irony, the humor was all over for him. Here was a woman, still young, sweet and kind, and gentle as a childish memory, with her fine eyes full of tears! That was bad enough. To make it worse, she went on to tell him of her son, him an outlaw, him a bushranger with a price upon his skin, as she might have outlined the case to a consulting physician. The boy had been born in the trouble of her early exile; he could not help his temperament. He had countless virtues; she extolled him in beaming parentheses. But he had too much imagination and too little balance. He was morbidly wrapped up in the whole subject of romantic crime, and no less than possessed with the personality of this one romantic criminal.

'I should be ashamed to tell you the childish lengths to which he has gone,' she went on, 'if he were quite himself on the point. But indeed he is not. He is Stingaree in his heart, Stingaree in his dreams; it is as debasing a form as mental and temperamental weakness could well take; yet I know, who watch over him half of the night. He has an eye-glass; he keeps revolvers; he has even bought a white mare! He can look extremely like the portraits one has seen of the wretched man. But come with me one moment.'

She took the lamp and led the way into the little room where Oswald Melvin slept. He had slept in it from that boyhood in which the brave woman had opened this sort of shop entirely for his sake. Music was his only talent; he was obviously not to be a genius in the musical world; but it was the only one in which she could foresee the selfish, self-willed child figuring with credit, and her foresight was only equalled by her resource. The business was ripe and ready for him when he grew up. And this was what he was making of it.

But Stingaree saw only the little bed that had once been far too large, the Bible still by its side, read or unread, the parents' portraits overhead. The mother was looking in an opposite direction; he followed her eyes, and there at the foot, where the infatuated fool could see it last thing at night and first in the morning, was an enlarged photograph of the bushranger himself.

It had been taken in audacious circumstances a year or two before. A travelling photographer had been one of yet another coach-load turned out and stood in a line by the masterful masterless man.

'Now you may take my photograph. The police refuse to know me when we do meet. Give them a chance.'

And he had posed on the spot with eye-glass up and pistols pointed, as he saw himself now, not less than a quarter life-size, in a great gaudy frame. But while he stared Mrs. Melvin had been rummaging in a drawer, and when he turned she was staring in her turn with glassy eyes. In her hands was an empty mahogany case with velvet moulds which ought to have been filled by a brace of missing revolvers.

'He kept it locked — he kept them in it!' she gasped. 'He may have done it this very night!'

'Done what?'

'Stuck up the Deniliquin mail. That is his maddest dream. I have heard him boast of it to his friends — the brainless boys who alone look up to him — I have even heard him rave of it in his dreams!'

Stingaree was heavy for a moment with a mental calculation. His head was a timetable of Cobb's coaches on the Riverina road-system; he nodded it as he located the imperilled vehicle.

'A dream it shall remain,' said he. 'But there's not a moment to lose!'

'Do you propose to follow and stop him?'

'If he really means it.'

'He may not. He will ride at night. He is often out as late.'

'Going and coming about the same time?'

'Yes — now I think of it.'

'Then his courage must have failed him hitherto, and it probably will again.'

'But if not!'

'I will cure him. But I must go at once. I have a horse not far away. I will gallop and meet the coach; if it is still safe, as you may be sure it will be, I shall scour the country for your son. I can tell him a fresh thing or two about Stingaree!'

'God bless you!'

'Leave him to me.'

'Oh, may God bless you always!'

His hands were in a lady's hands once more. Stingaree withdrew them gently. And he looked his last into the brave wet eyes raised gratefully to his.

The villain-worshipper was indeed duly posted in a certain belt of trees through which the coach-route ran, about half-way between the town and the first stage south. It was not his first nocturnal visit to the spot; often, as his prototype divined, had the mimic would-be desperado sat trembling on his hoary screw, revolvers ready, while the red eyes of the coach dilated down the road; and as often had the cumbrous ship pitched past unscathed. The week-kneed and weak-minded youth was too vain to feel much ashamed. He was biding his time, he could pick his night; one was too dark, another not dark enough; he had always some excuse for himself when he regained his room, still unstained by crime; and so the unhealthy excitement was deliciously maintained. To-night, as always when he sallied forth, the deed should be done; he only wished there was a shade less moon, and wondered whether he might not have done better to wait. But, as usual, the die was cast. And indeed it was quite a new complication that deterred this poor creature for the last time: he was feverishly expecting the coach when a patter of hoofs smote his ear from the opposite quarter.

This was enough to stay an older and a bolder hand. Oswald tucked in his guns with unrealized relief. It was his last instinct to wait and see whether the horseman was worth attacking for his own sake; he had room for few ideas at the same time; and his only new one was the sense of a new danger, which he prepared to meet by pocketing his pistols as a child bolts stolen fruit. There was no thinking before the act; but it was perhaps as characteristic of the naturally honest man as of the coward.

Stingaree swept through the trees at a gallop, the milk-white mare flashing in the moonlit patches. At the sight of her Oswald was convulsed with a premonition as to who was coming; his heart palpitated as even his heart had never done before; and yet he would have sat irresolute, inert, and let the man pass as he always let the coach, had the decision been left to him. The real milk-white mare affected the imitation in its turn as the coach-horses never had; and Oswald swayed and swam upon a whinnying steed . . .

'I thought you were Stingaree!'

The anti-climax was as profound as the weakling's relief. Yet there was a strong dash of indignation in his tone.

'What if I am?'

'But you're not. You're not half smart enough. You can't tell me anything about Stingaree!'

He put his eye-glass up with an air.

Stingaree put up his.

'You young fool!' said he.

The thoroughbred mare, the eye-glass, a peeping pistol, were all superfluous evidence. There was the far more unmistakable authority of voice and eye and bearing. Yet the voice at least was somehow familiar to the ear of Oswald, who stuttered as much when he was able.

'I must have heard it before, or have I dreamt it? I've thought a good deal about you, you know!'

To do him justice, he was no longer very nervous, though still physically shaken. On the other hand, he began already to feel the elation of his dreams.

'I do know. You've thought your soul into a pulp on the subject, and you must give it up,' said Stingaree, sternly.

Oswald sat aghast.

'But how on earth did you know?'

'I've come straight from your mother. You're breaking her heart.'

'But how can *you* have come straight from *her*?'

'I've come down for another melodeon. I've got to have one, too.'

'Another — '

And Oswald Melvin knew his drunken whim-driver for what he had really been.

'The yarn I told you about myself was true enough,' continued Stingaree. 'Only the names were altered, as they say; it happened to the other fellow, not to me. I made it happen. He is hardly likely to have lived to tell the tale.'

'Did he really try to betray you after what you'd done for him?'

'More or less. He looked on me as fair game.'

'But you had saved his life?'

Stingaree shrugged.

'We rode across him.'

'And you think he perished of dust and thirst?'

Stingaree nodded. 'In torment!'

'Then he got what he jolly well earned! Anything less would have been too good for him!' cried Oswald, and with a boyish, uncompromising heat which spoke to some human nature in him still.

But Stingaree frowned up the moonlit track. There was still no sign of the coach. Yet time was short, and the morbid enthusiast was not to be disgusted; indeed, he was all enthusiasm now, and a less unattractive lad than the bushranger had hoped to find him. He looked the white screw and Oswald up and down as they sat in their saddles in the moonshine: it seemed like sunlight on that beaming fool.

'And you think of commencing bushranger, do you?'

'Rather!'

'It's a hard life while it lasts, and a nasty death to top up with.'

'They don't hang you for it.'

'They might hang me for the man I put back in the vile dust from whence he sprung. They'd hang you in six months. You've too many nerves. You'd pull the trigger every time.'

'A short life and a merry one!' cried the reckless Oswald. 'I shouldn't care.'

'But your mother would,' retorted Stingaree, sharply. 'Don't think about yourself so much; think about her for a change.'

The young man turned dusky in the moonlight; he was wounded where the Bishop had wounded him, and Stingaree was quick to see it — as quick to turn the knife round in the wound.

'What a bushranger!' he jeered. 'Put your plucky little mother in a side-saddle and she'd make two of you — ten of you — twenty of a puny, namby-pamby, conceited young idiot like you! Upon my word, Melvin, if I had a mother like you I should be ashamed of myself. I never had, I may tell you, or I shouldn't have come down to a dog's life like this.'

The bushranger paused to watch the effect of his insults. It was not quite what he wanted. The youth would not hang his head. And, if he did not answer back, he looked back doggedly enough; for he could be dogged, in a passive way; it was his one hard quality, the knot in a character of green deal. Stingaree glanced up the road once more, but only for an instant.

'It is a dog's life,' he went on, 'whether you believe it or not. But it takes a bull-dog to live it, and don't you forget it. It's no life for a young poodle like you! You can't stick up a better man than yourself, not more than once or twice. It requires something more than a six-shooter, and a good deal more than was put into you, my son! But you shall see for yourself; look over your shoulder.'

Oswald did so, and started in a fashion that set the bushranger nodding his scorn. It was only a pair of lamps still close together in the distance up the road.

'The coach!' exclaimed the excited youth.

'Exactly,' said Stingaree, 'and I'm going to stick it up.'

Excitement grew to frenzy in a flash.

'I'll help you!'

'You'll do no such thing. But you shall see how it's done, and then ask yourself candidly if it's nice work and if you're the man to do it. Ride a hundred yards further in, tether your horse quickly in the thickest scrub you can find, then run back and climb into the fork of this gum-tree. You'll have time; if you're sharp I'll give you a leg up. But I sha'n't be surprised if I don't see you again!'

There is no saying what Oswald might have done, but for these last words. Certain it is that they set him galloping with an oath, and brought him back panting in another minute. The coach-lamps were not much wider apart. Stingaree awaited him, also on foot, and quicker than the telling Oswald was ensconced on high where he could see through the meagre drooping leaves with very little danger of being seen.

'And if you come down before I'm done and gone — if it's not to glory — I'll run some lead through you! You'll be the first!'

Oswald perched reflecting on this final threat; and the scene soon enacted before his eyes was viewed as usual through the aura of his own egoism. He longed all the time to be taking part in it; he could see himself so distinctly at the work — save for about a minute in the middle, when for once in his life he held his breath and trembled for other skins.

There had been no unusual feature. The life-size coach-lamps had shown their mountain-range of outside passengers against moonlit sky or trees. A cigar paled and reddened between the teeth of one, plain wreaths of smoke floated from his lips, with but an instant's break when Stingaree rode out and stopped the coach. The three leaders reared; the two wheelers were pulled almost to their haunches. The driver was docile in deed, though profane in word; and Stingaree himself discovered a horrifying vocabulary out of keeping with his reputation. In incredibly few minutes driver and passengers were formed in a line and robbed in rotation, all but two ladies who were kept inside unmolested. A flagrant Irishman declared it was the proudest day of his life, and Oswald's heart went out to him, though it rather displeased him to find his own sentiments shared by the vulgar. The man with the cigar kept it glowing all the time. The mail-bags were not demanded on this occasion. Stingaree had no time to waste on them. He was still collecting purse and watch, when Oswald's young blood froze in the stiffening limbs he dared not move.

One of the ladies had got down from the coach on the off side, and behold! it was a man wrapped in a rug, which dropped from him as he crept round behind the horses. At their head stood the lily mare, as if doing her own nefarious part by her own kind. In a twinkling the mad adventurer was on her back, and all this time Oswald longed to jump down, or at least to shout a warning to his hero, but, as usual, his desires were unproductive of word or deed. And then Stingaree saw his man.

He did not fire; he did not shift sight or barrel for a moment from the docile file before him. 'Barmaid! Barmaid, my pet!' he cried, and hardly looked to see what happened.

But Oswald watched the mare stop, prick her ears under the hammering of unspurred heels, spin round, bucking as she spun, and toss her rider like a bull. There in the moonlight he lay like lead, with leaden face upturned to the shuddering youngster in the tree.

'One of you a doctor?' asked Stingaree, checking a forward movement of the file.

'I am.'

The cigar was paling between finger and thumb.

'Then come you here and have a look at him. The rest of you move at your peril!'

Stingaree led the way, stepping backward, but not as far as the injured man, who sat up ruefully as the bushranger sprang into the saddle.

'Another yard, and I'd have grabbed your ankles!' said the man on the ground.

'You're a stout fellow, but I know more about this game than you,' the outlaw answered, riding to his distance and reining up. 'If I didn't you might have had me — but you must think of something better for Stingaree!'

He galloped his mare into the bush and Oswald clung in lonely terror to his tree. A snatch of conversation called him to attention. The plundered party were clambering philosophically to their seats, while the driver blasphemed delightedly over the integrity of his mails.

'That wasn't Stingaree,' said one.

'You bet it was!'

'How much? He hardly ever works so far south.'

'And he's nuts on mails.'

'But if it wasn't Stingaree, who was it?'

'It was him all right. Look at the mare.'

'She isn't the only white 'orse ever foaled,' remarked the driver, sorting his fistful of reins.

'But who else could it have been?'

The driver uttered an inspired imprecation.

'I can tell you. I chanst to live in this here township we're comin' to. On second thoughts, I'll keep it to myself till we get there.'

And he cracked his whip.

Oswald himself rode back to the township before the moon went down. He was very heavy with his own reflections. How magnificent! It had all surpassed his most extravagant imaginings — in audacity, in expedition, in simple mastery of the mutable many by the dominant one. He forgave Stingaree his gibes and insults; he could have forgiven a horse-whipping from that king of men. Stingaree had been his imaginary god before; he was a realized ideal from this night forth, and the reality outdid the dream.

But the fly of self must always poison this young man's ointment, and to-night there was some excuse from his degenerate point of view. He must give it up. Stingaree was right; it was only one man in thousands who could do unerringly what he had done that night. Oswald Melvin was not that man. He saw it for himself at last. But it was a bitter hour for him. Life in the music-shop would fall very flat after this; he would be dishonored before his only friends, the unworthy hobbledehoys who were to have joined his gang; he could not tell them what had happened, not at least until he had invented some less inglorious part for himself, and that was a difficulty in view of newspaper reports of the sticking-up. He could scarcely tell them a true word of what had passed between himself and Stingaree. If only he might yet grow more like the master! If only he might still hope to follow so sublime a lead!

Thus aspiring, vainly as now he knew, Oswald Melvin rode slowly back into the excited town, and past the lighted police-barracks, in the innocence of that portion of his heart. But one had flown like the wind ahead of him, and two in uniform, followed by that one, dashed out on Oswald and the old white screw.

'Surrender!' sang out one.

'In the Queen's name!' added the other.

'Call yourself Stingaree!' panted the runner.

Our egoist was quick enough to grasp their meaning, but quicker still to see and to seize the chance of a crazy lifetime. Always acute where his own vanity was touched, his promptitude was for once on a par with his perceptions.

'Had your eye on me long?' he inquired, delightfully, as he dismounted.

'Long enough,' said one policeman. The other was busy plucking loaded revolvers from the desperado's pockets. A crowd had formed.

'If you're looking for the loot,' he went on, raising his voice for the benefit of all, 'you may look. *I* sha'n't tell you, and it'll take you all your time!'

But a surprise was in store for prisoner and police alike. Every stolen watch and all the missing money were discovered no later than next morning in the bush quite close to the scene of the outrage. There had been no attempt to hide them; they lay in a heap, dumped from the saddle, with no more depreciation than a broken watch-glass. True to his new character, Oswald learned this development without flinching. His ready comment was in next day's papers.

'There was nothing worth having,' he had maintained, and did not see the wisdom of the boast until a lawyer called and pointed out that it contained the nucleus of a strong defence.

'I'll defend myself, thank you,' said the inflated fool.

'Then you'll make a mess of it, and deserve all you get. And it would be a pity to spoil such a good defence.'

'What is the defence?'

'You did it for a joke, of course!'

Oswald smiled inscrutably, and dismissed his visitor with a lordly promise to consider the proposition and that lawyer's claims upon the case. Never was such triumph tasted in guilty immunity as was this innocent man's under cloud of guilt so apparent as to impose on every mind. He had but carried out a notorious intention; for his few friends were the first to betray their captain, albeit his bold bearing and magnanimous smiles won an admiration which they had never before vouchsafed him in their hearts. He was, indeed, a different man. He had lived to see Stingaree in action, and now he modelled himself from the life. The only doubt was as to whether at the last of that business he had actually avowed himself Stingaree or not. There might have been trouble about the horse, but fortunately for the enthusiastic prisoner the man who had been thrown was allowed to proceed on a pressing journey to the Barcoo. There was a plethora of evidence without his; besides, the hide-and-bone mare was called Barmaid, after the original, and it was known that Oswald had tried to teach the old creature tricks; above all, the prisoner had never pretended to deny his guilt. Still, this matter of the horses gave him a certain sense of insecurity in his cosy cell.

He had awakened to find himself not only deliciously notorious, but actually more of a man than in his heart of hearts he had dared to hope. The tenacity and consistency of his pose were alike remarkable. Even in the overweening cause of egoism he had never shown so much character in his life. Yet he shuddered to realize that, given the usual time for reflection before his great moment, that moment might have proved as mean as many another when the spirit had been wine and the flesh water. There was, in fine, but one feature of the affair which even Oswald Melvin, drunk with notoriety and secretly sanguine of a nominal punishment, could not contemplate with absolute satisfaction. But that feature followed the others into the papers which kept him intoxicated. And a bundle of these papers found their adventurous way to the latest fastness of Stingaree in the mallee.

The real villain dropped his eye-glass, clapped it in again, and did his best to crack it with his stare. Student of character as he was, he could not have conceived such a development in such a character. He read on, more enlightened than amused. 'To think he had the pluck!' he murmured, as he dropped that *Australasian* and took up the next week's. He was filled with admiration, but soon a frown and then an oath came to put an end to it. 'The little beast,' he cried, 'he'll kill that woman! He can't have kept it up.' He sorted the papers for the latest of all — a sinful publican saved them for him — and therein read that Oswald Melvin had been committed for trial, and that his only concern was for the condition of his mother, which was still unchanged, and had seemed latterly to distress the prisoner very much.

'I'll distress him!' roared Stingaree to the mallee. 'I'll distress him, if we change places for it!'

Riding all night, and as much as he dared by day, it was some hundred hours before he paid his third and last visit to the Melvins' music-shop. He rode boldly to the door, but he rode a piebald mare not to be confused in the most suspicious mind with the no more conspicuous Barmaid. It is true the brown parts smelt of Condy's Fluid, and were at once strange and seemingly a little tender to the touch. But Stingaree allowed no meddling with his mount; and only a very sinful publican, very many leagues back, was in the secret.

There were no lighted windows behind the shop to-night. The whole place was in darkness, and Stingaree knocked in vain. A neighbor appeared upon the next veranda.

'Who is it you want?' he asked.

'Mrs. Melvin.'

'It's no use knocking for her.'

'Is she dead?'

'Not that I know of; but she can't be long for this world.'

'Where is she now?'

'Bishop's Lodge; they say Miss Methuen's with her day and night.'

For it was in the days of the Bishop's daughter, who had a strong mind but no sense of humor, and a heart only fickle in its own affairs. Miss Methuen made an admirable, if a somewhat too assiduous and dictatorial, nurse. She had, however, a fund of real sympathy with the afflicted, and Mrs. Melvin's only serious complaint (which she intended to die without uttering) was that she was never left alone with her grief by day or night. It was Miss Methuen who, sitting with rather ostentatious patience in the dark, at the open window, until her patient should fall or pretend to be asleep, saw a man ride a piebald horse in at the gate, and then, half-way up the drive, suspiciously dismount and lead his horse into a tempting shrubbery.

Stingaree did not often change his mind at the last moment, but he knew the man on whose generosity he was about to throw himself, which was to know further that that generosity would be curbed by judgment, and to reflect that he was least likely to be deprived of a horse whose whereabouts was known only to himself. There was but one lighted room when he eventually stole upon the house; it had a veranda to itself; and in the bright frame of the French windows, which stood open, sat the Bishop with his Bible on his knees.

'Yes, I know you,' said he, putting his marker in the place as Stingaree entered, boots in one hand and something else in the other. 'I thought we should meet again. Do you mind putting that thing back in your pocket?'

'Will you promise not to call a soul?'

'Oh, dear, yes.'

'You weren't expecting me, were you?' cried Stingaree, suspiciously.

'I've been expecting you for months,' returned the Bishop. 'You knew my address, but I hadn't yours. We were bound to meet again.'

Stingaree smiled as he took his revolver by the barrel and carried it across the room to Dr. Methuen.

'What's that for? I don't want it; put it in your own pocket. At least I can trust you not to take my life in cold blood.'

The Bishop seemed nettled and annoyed. Stingaree loved him.

'I don't come to take anything, much less life,' he said. 'I come to save it; if it is not too late.'

'To save life — here?'

'In your house.'

'But whom do you know of my household?'

'Mrs. Melvin. I have had the honor of meeting her twice, though each time she was unaware of the dishonor of meeting me. The last time I promised to try to save her unhappy son from himself. I found him waiting to waylay the coach, told him who I was, and had ten minutes to try to cure him in. He wouldn't listen to reason; insult ran like water off his back. I did my best to show him what a life it was he longed to lead, and how much more there was in it than a loaded revolver. He wouldn't take my word for it, however, so I put him out of harm's way, up in a tree; and when the coach came along I gave him as brutal an exhibition of the art of bushranging as I could without spilling blood. I promise you it was for no other reason. What did I want with watches? What were a few pounds to me? I dropped the lot that the lad might know.'

The Bishop started to his gaitered legs.

'And he's actually innocent all the time?'

'Of the deed, as the babe unborn.'

'Then why in the wide world — '

Dr. Methuen stood beggared of further speech. His mind was too plain and sane for immediate understanding of such a type as Oswald Melvin. But the bushranger hit off that young man's character in half-a-dozen trenchant phrases.

'He must be let out, and it may save his mother's life; but if he were mine,' exclaimed the Bishop, 'I would rather he had done the other deed! But what about you?' he added, suddenly, his eyes resting on his sardonic visitor, who had disguised himself far less than his horse. 'It will mean giving yourself up.'

'No. You know me. You can spread what I've told you.'

The Bishop shifted uneasily on his hearth-rug.

'I may not see my way to that,' said he. 'Besides, you must have run a lot of risks to do this good action; how do you know you haven't been recognized already? I should have known you anywhere.'

'But you have undertaken not to raise an alarm, my lord.'

'I shall not break my promise.'

There was a grim regret in the Bishop's voice. Stingaree thought he understood it.

'Thank you,' he said.

'Don't thank me, pray!' Dr. Methuen could be quite testy on occasion. 'I have other duties than to you, you know, and I only answer for my actions during the actual period of our interview. There are many things I should like to say to you, my brother,' a gentler voice went on, 'but this is hardly the time for me to say them. But there is one question I should like to ask you for the peace of both our souls, and for the maintenance of my own belief in human nature.' He threw up an episcopal hand dramatically. 'If you earnestly and honestly wished to save this poor lady's life, and there were no other way, would you then be man enough to give yourself up — to give your liberty for her life?'

Stingaree took time to think. His eyes were brightly fixed upon the Bishop's. Yet they saw a little bedroom just as plain, an English lady standing by the empty bed, and at its foot a portrait of himself armed to the teeth.

'For hers?' said he. 'Yes, like a shot!'

'I'm thankful to hear it,' replied the Bishop, with most fervent relief. 'I only wish you could have the opportunity. But now you never will. My brother, if you look round, you will see why!'

Stingaree looked round without a word. In the Bishop's eyes at the last instant he had learned what to expect. A firing-party of four stocking-soled constables were drawn across the opened French windows, their levelled rifles poking through.

The bushranger looked over his shoulder with a bitter smile. 'You've done me, after all!' said he, and stretched out empty hands.

'It was done before I saw you,' the Bishop made answer. 'I had already sent for the police.'

One had entered excitedly by an inner door.

'And he didn't do you at all!' cried the voice of high hysteria. 'It was I who saw you — it was I who guessed who it was! Oh, father, why have you been talking so long to such a dreadful man? I made sure he would shoot you, and you'd still be shot if they had to shoot him! Move — move — move!'

Stingaree looked at the strong-minded girl, shrill with her triumph, quite carried away by her excitement, all undaunted by the prospect of bloodshed before her eyes. And it was he who moved, with but a shrug of the shoulders, and gave himself up without another sign.

The Moth and the Star

I

Darlinghurst Jail had never immured a more interesting prisoner than the back-block bandit who was tried and convicted under the strange style and title which he had made his own. Not even in prison was his real name ever known, and the wild speculations of some imaginative officials were nothing else up to the end. There was enough color in their wildness, however, to crown the convict with a certain halo of romance, which his behavior in jail did nothing to dispel. That, of course, was exemplary, since Stingaree had never been a fool; but it was something more and rarer. Not content simply to follow the line of least resistance, he exhibited from the first a spirit and a philosophy unique indeed beneath the broad arrow. And so far from decreasing with the years of his captivity, these attractive qualities won him friend after friend among the officials, and privilege upon privilege at their hands, while amply justifying the romantic interest in his case.

At last there came to Sydney a person more

247

capable of an acute appreciation of the heroic villain than his most ardent admirer on the spot. Lucius Brady was a long-haired Irishman of letters, bard and bookworm, rebel and reviewer; in his ample leisure he was also the most enthusiastic criminologist in London. And as President of an exceedingly esoteric Society for the Cultivation of Criminals, even from London did he come for a prearranged series of interviews with the last and the most distinguished of all the bushrangers.

It was to Lucius Brady, his biographer to be, that Stingaree confided the data of all the misdeeds recounted in these pages; but of his life during the quiet intervals, of his relations with confederates, and his more honest dealings with honest folk (of which many a pretty tale was rife), he was not to be persuaded to speak without an irritating reserve.

'Keep to my points of contact with the world, about which something is known already, and you shall have the whole truth of each matter,' said the convict. 'But I don't intend to give away the altogether unknown, and I doubt if it would interest you if I did. The most interesting thing to me has been the different types with whom I have had what it pleases you to term professional relations, and the very different ways in which they have taken me. You read character by flashlight along the barrel of your revolver. What you should do is to hunt up my various victims and get at their point of view; you really mustn't press me to hark back to mine. As it is you bring a whiff of the outer world which makes me bruise my wings against the bars.'

The criminologist gloated over such speeches from such lips. It would have touched another to note what an irresistible fascination the bars had for the wings, despite all pain; but Lucius Brady's interest in Stingaree was exclusively intellectual. His heart never ached for a roving spirit in confinement; it did not occur to him to suppress a detail of his own days in Sydney, down to the attractions of an Italian restaurant he had discovered near the jail, the flavor of the Chianti and so forth. On the contrary, it was most interesting to note the play of features in the tortured man, who after all brought his torture on himself by asking so many questions. Soon, when his visitor left him, the bondman could follow the free in all but the flesh, through every corridor of the prison and every street outside, to the hotel where you read the English papers on the veranda, or to the little restaurant where the Chianti was corked with oil which the waiter removed with a wisp of tow.

One day, late in the afternoon, as Lucius Brady was beaming on him through his spectacles, and indulging in an incisive criticism on the champagne at Government House, Stingaree quietly garroted him. A gag was in all readiness, likewise strips of coarse sheeting torn up for the purpose in the night. Black in the face, but with breath still in his body, the criminologist was carefully gagged and tied down to the bedstead, while his living image (at a casual glance) strolled with bent head, black sombrero, spectacles and frock-coat, first through the cold corridors and presently along the streets.

The heat of the pavement striking to his soles was the first of a hundred exquisite sensations; but Stingaree did not permit himself to savor one of them. Indeed, he had his work cut out to check the pace his heart dictated; and it was by admirable exercise of the will that he wandered along, deep to all appearance in a Camelot Classic which he had found in the criminologist's pocket; in reality blinded by the glasses, but all the more vigilant out of the corners of his eyes.

A suburb was the scene of these perambulations; had he but dared to lift his face, Stingaree might have caught a glimpse of the bluest of blue water; and his prison eyes hungered for the sight, but he would not raise his eyes so long as footsteps sounded on the same pavement. By taking judicious turnings, however, he drifted into a quiet road, with gray suburban bungalows on one side and building lots on the other. No step approached. He could look up at last. And the very bungalow that he was passing was shut up, yet furnished; the people had merely gone away, servants and all; he saw it at a glance from the newspapers plastering the windows which caught the sun. In an instant he was in the garden, and in another he had forced a side gate leading by an alley to backyard and kitchen door; but for many minutes he went no further than this gate, behind which he cowered, prepared with excuses in case he had already been observed.

It was in this interval that Stingaree recalled the season with a thrill; for it was Christmas week, and without a doubt the house would be empty till the New Year. Here was one port for the storm that must follow his escape. And a very pleasant port he found it on entering, after due precautionary delay.

Clearly the abode of young married people, the bungalow was fitted and furnished with a taste which appealed almost painfully to Stingaree; the drawing-room was draped in sheets, but the walls carried a few good

251

engravings, some of which he remembered with a stab. It was the dressing-room, however, that he wanted, and the dressing-room made him rub his hands. The dainty establishment had no more luxurious corner, what with the fitted bath, circular shaving-glass, packed trouser-press, a row of boots on trees, and a fine old wardrobe full of hanging coats. Stingaree began by selecting his suit; and it may have been his vanity, or a strange longing to look for once what he once had been, but he could not resist the young man's excellent evening clothes.

'This fellow comes from Home,' said he. 'And they are spending their Christmas pretty far back, or he would have taken these with him.'

He had wallowed in the highly enamelled bath, and was looking for a towel when he saw his head in the shaving-glass; he was dry enough before he could think of anything else. There was a dilemma, obvious yet unforeseen. That shaven head! Purple and fine linen could not disguise the convict's crop; a wig was the only hope; but to wear a wig one must first try it on — and let the perruquier call the police. The knot was Gordian. And yet, desperately as Stingaree sought unravelment, he was at the same time subconsciously as deep in a study of a face so unfamiliar that at first he had scarcely known it for his own. It was far leaner than of old; it was no longer richly tanned; and the mouth called louder than ever for a mustache. The hair, what there was of it, seemed iron-gray. It had certainly receded at the temples. What a pity, while it was about it —

Stingaree clapped his hands; his hunt for the razor was feverish, tremulous. Such a young man must have many razors; he had, he had — here they were. Oh, young man blessed among young men!

It was quite dark when a gentleman in evening clothes, light overcoat, and opera hat, sallied forth into the quiet road. Quiet as it was, however, a whistle blew as he trod the pavement, and his hour or two of liberty seemed at an end. His long term in prison had mixed Stingaree's ideas of the old country and the new; he had forgotten that it is the postmen who blow the whistles in Australia. Yet this postman stopped him on the spot.

'Beg your pardon, sir, but if it's quite convenient may I ask you for the Christmas-box you was kind enough to promise me?'

'I think you are mistaking me for someone else,' said Stingaree.

'Why, so I am, sir! I thought you came out of Mr. Brinton's house.'

'Sorry to disappoint you,' said the convict. 'If I only had change you should have some of it, in spite of your mistake; but, unfortunately, I have none.'

He had, however, a handsome pair of opera-glasses, which he converted into change (on the gratuitous plea that he had forgotten his purse) at the first pawnbroker's on the confines of the city. The pawnbroker talked Greek to him at once.

'It's a pity you won't be able to see 'er, sir, as well as 'ear 'er,' said he.

'Perhaps they have them on hire in the theatre,' replied Stingaree at a venture. The pawnbroker's face instantly advised him that his observation was wide of the obscure mark.

'The theatre! You won't 'ear 'er at any theatre in Sydney, nor yet in the Southern 'Emisphere. Town 'Alls is the only lay for 'Ilda Bouverie out 'ere!'

At first the name conveyed nothing to Stingaree. Yet it was not wholly unfamiliar.

'Of course,' said he. 'The Town Hall I meant.'

The pawnbroker leered as he put down a sovereign and a shilling.

'What a season she's 'aving, sir!'

'Ah! What a season!'

And Stingaree wagged his opera-hatted head.

"'Undreds of pounds' worth of flowers flung on to every platform, and not a dry eye in the place!'

'I know,' said the feeling Stingaree.

'It's wonderful to think of this 'ere Colony prodoocin' the world's best primer donner!'

'It is, indeed.'

'When you think of 'er start.'

'That's true.'

The pawnbroker leant across his counter and leered more than ever in his customer's face.

'They say she ain't no better than she ought to be!'

'Really?'

'It's right, too; but what can you expect of a primer donner whose fortune was made by a blood-thirsty bushranger like that there Stingaree?'

'You little scurrilous wretch!' cried the bushranger, and flung out of the shop that second.

It was a miracle. He remembered everything now. Then he had done the world a service as well as the woman! He gave thanks for the guinea in his pocket, and asked his way to the Town Hall. And as he marched down the middle of the lighted streets the first flock of newsboys came flying in his face.

'*Escape of Stingaree! Escape of Stingaree!*

*Cowardly Outrage on Famous Author!
Escape of Stingaree!!'*

The damp pink papers were in the hands of
the overflow crowd outside the hall; his own
name was already in every mouth, continually
coupled with that of the world-renowned
Hilda Bouverie. It did not deter the convict
from elbowing his way through the mass that
gloated over his deed exactly as they would
have gloated over his destruction on the
gallows. 'I have my ticket; I have been
detained,' he told the police; and at the last
line of defence he whispered, 'A guinea for
standing-room!' And the guinea got it.

It was the interval between parts one and
two. He thought of that other interval, when
he had made such a different entry at the
same juncture; the other concert-room would
have gone some fifty times into this. All at
once fell a hush, and then a rising thunder of
applause, and some one requested Stingaree
to remove his hat; he did so, and a cold
creeping of the shaven flesh reminded him of
his general position and of this particular
peril. But no one took any notice of him or of
his head. And it was not Hilda Bouverie this
time; it was a pianiste in violent magenta and
elaborate lace, whose performance also was
loud and embroidered. Followed a beautiful
young baritone whom Miss Bouverie had

brought from London in her pocket for the tour. He sang three little songs very charmingly indeed; but there was no encore. The gods were burning for their own; perfunctory plaudits died to a dramatic pause.

And then, and then, amid deafening salvos a dazzling vision appeared upon the platform, came forward with the carriage of a conscious queen, stood bowing and beaming in the gloss and glitter of fabric and of gem that were yet less radiant than herself. Stingaree stood inanimate between stamping feet and clapping hands. No; he would never have connected this magnificent woman with the simple bush girl in the unpretentious frocks that he recalled as clearly as her former self. He had looked for less finery, less physical development, less, indeed, of the grand operatic *tout-ensemble*. But acting ended with her smile, and much of the old innocent simplicity came back as the lips parted in song. And her song had not been spoilt by riches and adulation; her song had not sacrificed sweetness to artifice; there was even more than the old magic in her song.

'Is this a dream?
Then waking would be pain!

257

Oh! do not wake me;
   Let me dream again.'

It was no new number even then; even Stingaree had often heard it, and heard great singers go the least degree flat upon the first 'dream.' He listened critically. Hilda Bouverie was not one of the delinquents. Her intonation was as perfect as that of the great violinists, her high notes had the rarefied quality of the E string finely touched. It was a flawless, if a purely popular, performance; and the musical heart of one listener in that crowded room was too full for mere applause. But he waited with patient curiosity for the encore, waited while courtesy after courtesy was given in vain. She had to yield; she yielded with a winning grace. And the first bars of the new song set one full heart beating, so that the earlier words were lost upon his brain.

'She ran before me in the meads;
   And down this world-worn track
She leads me on; but while she leads
   She never gazes back.

'And yet her voice is in my dreams,
   To witch me more and more;

That wooing voice! Ah me, it seems
　　Less near me than of yore.

'Lightly I sped when hope was high,
　　And youth beguiled the chase;
I follow — follow still; but I
　　Shall never see her Face.'

So the song ended; and in the ultimate quiet the need of speech came over Stingaree.

'"The Unrealized Ideal," he informed a neighbor.

'Rather!' rejoined the man, treating the stale news as a mere remark. 'We never let her off without that.'

'I suppose not,' said Stingaree.

'It's the song the bushranger forced her to sing at the back-block concert, and it made her fortune! Good old Stingaree! By the way, I heard somebody behind me say he had escaped. That can't be true?'

'The newsboys were yelling it as I came along late.'

'Well,' said Stingaree's neighbor, 'if he has escaped, and I for one don't hope he hasn't, this is where he ought to be. Just the sort of thing he'd do, too. Good old sportsman, Stingaree!'

It was an embarrassing compliment, eye to eye and foot to foot, wedged in a crowd.

The bushranger did not fish for any more; neither did he wait to hear Hilda Bouverie sing again, though this cost him much. But he had one more word with his neighbor before he went.

'You don't happen to know where she's staying, I suppose? I've met her once or twice, and I might call.'

The other smiled as on some suicidal moth.

'There's only one place good enough for a star like her in Sydney.'

'And that is?'

'Government House.'

II

His Excellency of the moment was a young nobleman of sporting proclivities and your true sportsman's breadth of mind. He was immensely popular with all sects and sections but the aggressively puritanical and the narrowly austere. He graced the theatre with his constant presence, the Turf with his own horses. His entertainment was lavish, and in quality far above the gubernatorial average. Late life and soul of exalted circle, he was hide-bound by few of the conventional trammels that distinguished the older type of peer to which the

Colonies had been accustomed. It was the obvious course for such a Governor and his kindred lady to insist upon making the great Miss Bouverie their guest for the period of her professional sojourn in the capital; and a semi-Bohemian supper at the Government House was but a characteristic *finale* to her first great concert.

The *prima donna* sat on the Governor's right, and at the proper point his Excellency sang her praises in a charmingly informal speech, which delighted and amused the press men, actors and actresses whom he had collected for the occasion. Only the guest of honor looked a little weary and condescending; she had a sufficient experience of such entertainments in London, where the actors were all London actors, the authors and journalists men whose names one knew. Mere peers were no great treat either; in a word, Hilda Bouverie was not a little spoilt. She had lost the girl's glad outlook on the world, which some women keep until old age. There were stories about her which would have accounted for a deeper deterioration. Yet she was the Governor's guest, and her behavior not unworthy of the honor. On him at least she smiled, and her real smile, less expansive than the platform counterfeit, had still its genuine sweetness, its winning flashes; and, at its worst, it was more sad than bitter.

To-night the woman was an exhausted artist — unnerved, unstrung, unfitted for the world, yet only showing it in a languid appreciation which her host and hostess were the first to understand. Indeed, it was the great lady who carried her off, bowing with her platform bow, and smiling that smile, before the banquet was at an end.

A charming suite of rooms had been placed at the disposal of the *prima donna*; the boudoir was like a hot-house with the floral offerings of the evening, already tastefully arranged by madame's own Swiss maid. But the weary lady walked straight through to her bedroom, and sank with a sigh into the arm-chair before the glass.

'Who brought this?' she asked, peevishly picking a twisted note from amid the golden furniture of her toilet-table.

'I never saw it until this minute, madame!' the Swiss maid answered, in dismay. 'It was not there ten minutes ago, I am sure, madame!'

'Where have you been since?'

'Down to the servants' hall, for one minute, madame.'

Miss Bouverie read the note, and was an

animated being in three seconds. She looked in the glass, the flush became her, and even as she looked all horror died in her dark-blue eyes. Instead there came a glitter that warned the maid.

'I am tired of you, Lea,' cried madame. 'You let people bring notes into my room, and you say you were only out of it a minute. Be good enough to leave me for the night. I can look after myself, for once!'

The maid protested, wept, but was expelled, and a key turned between them; then Hilda Bouverie read her note again: —

'Escaped this afternoon. Came to your concert. Hiding in boudoir. Give me five minutes, or raise alarm, which you please.

— STINGAREE.'

So ran his words in pencil on her own paper, and they were true; she had heard at supper of the escape. Once more she looked in the glass. And to her own eyes in these minutes she looked years younger — there was a new sensation left in life!

A touch to her hair, a glance in the pier-glass, and all for a notorious convict broken prison! So into the boudoir with her grandest air; but again she locked the door behind her, and, sweeping round, beheld a bald man bowing to her in immaculate evening clothes.

'Are you the writer of a note found on my dressing-table?' she demanded, every syllable off the ice.

'I am.'

'Then who are you, besides being an impudent forger?'

'You name the one crime I never committed,' said he. 'I am Stingaree.'

And they gazed into each other's eyes; but not yet were hers to be believed.

'He only escaped this afternoon!'

'I am he.'

'With a bald head?'

'Thanks to a razor.'

'And in those clothes?'

'I found them where I found the razor. Look; they don't fit me as well as they might.'

And he drew nearer, flinging out an abbreviated sleeve; but she looked all the harder in his face.

'Yes. I begin to remember your face; but it has changed.'

'It has gazed on prison walls for many years.'

'I heard . . . I was grieved . . . but it was bound to come.'

'It may come again. I care very little, after this!'

And his dark eyes shone, his deep voice vibrated; then he glanced over a shrugged shoulder toward the outer door, and Hilda darted as if to turn that key too, but there was none to turn.

'It ought to happen at once,' she said, 'and through me.'

'But it will not.'

His assurance annoyed her; she preferred his homage.

'I know what you mean,' she cried. 'You did me a service years ago. I am not to forget it!'

'It is not I who have kept it before your mind.'

'Perhaps not; but that's why you come to me to-night.'

Stingaree looked upon the spirited, spoilt beauty in her satin and diamonds and pearls; villain as he was, he held himself at her mercy, but he was not going to kneel to her for that. He saw a woman who had heard the truth from very few men, a nature grown in mastery as his own had inevitably shrunk: it was worth being at large to pit the old Adam still remaining to him against the old Eve in this petted darling of the world. But false protestations were no counters in his game.

'Miss Bouverie,' said Stingaree, 'you may

well suppose that I have borne you in mind all these years. As a matter of honest fact, when I first heard your name this evening, I was slow to connect it with any human being. You look angry. I intend no insult. If you have not forgotten the life I was leading before, you would very readily understand that I have never heard your name from those days to this. That is my misfortune, if also my own fault. It should suffice that, when I did remember, I came at my peril to hear you sing, and that before I dreamt of coming an inch further. But I heard them say, both in the hall and outside, that you owed your start to me; now one thinks of it, it must have been a rather striking advertisement; and I reflected that not another soul in Sydney can possibly owe me anything at all. So I came straight to you, without thinking twice about it. Criminal as I have been, and am, my one thought was and is that I deserve some little consideration at your hands.'

'You mean money?'

'I have not a penny. It would make all the difference to me. And I give you my word, if that is any satisfaction to you, I would be an honest man from this time forth!'

'You actually ask me to assist a criminal and escaped convict — me, Hilda Bouverie, at my own absolute risk!'

'I took a risk for you nine years ago, Miss Bouverie; it was all I did take,' said Stingaree, 'at the concert that made your name.'

'And you rub it in,' she told him. 'You rub it in!'

'I am running for my life!' he exclaimed, in answer. 'It wouldn't have been necessary — that would have been enough for the Miss Bouverie I knew then. But you are different; you are another being, you are a woman of the world; your heart, your heart is dead and gone!'

He cut her to it, none the less; he could not have inflicted a deeper wound. The blood leapt to her face and neck; she cried out at the insult, the indignity, the outrage of it all; and crying she darted to the door.

It was locked.

She turned on Stingaree.

'You dared to lock the door — you dared! Give me the key this instant.'

'I refuse.'

'Very well! You have heard my voice; you shall hear it again!'

Her pale lips made the perfect round, her grand teeth gleamed in the electric light.

He arrested her, not with violence, but a shrug.

'I shall jump out of the window and break my neck. They don't take me twice — alive.'

She glared at him in anger and contempt. He meant it. Then let him do it. Her eyes told him all that; but as they flashed, stabbing him, their expression altered, and in a trice her ear was to the keyhole.

'Something has happened,' she whispered, turning a scared face up to him. 'I hear your name. They have traced you here. They are coming! Oh! what are we to do?'

He strode over to the door.

'If you fear a scandal I can give myself up this moment and explain all.'

He spoke eagerly. The thought was sudden. She rose up, looking in his eyes.

'No, you shall not,' she said. Her hand flew out behind her, and in two seconds the brilliant room had click-clicked into a velvet darkness.

'Stand like a mouse,' she whispered, and he heard her reach the inner door, where she stood like another.

Steps and voices came along the landing at a quick crescendo.

'Miss Bouverie! Miss Bouverie! Miss Bouverie!'

It was his Excellency's own gay voice. And it continued until with much noise Miss Bouverie flung her bedroom door wide open, put on the light within, ran across the boudoir, put on the boudoir light, and stooped to parley through the keyhole.

'The bushranger Stingaree has been traced to Government House.'

'Good heavens!'

'One of your windows was seen open.'

'He had not come in through it.'

'Then you were heard raising your voice.'

'That was to my maid. This is all through her. I don't know how to tell you, but she leaves me in the morning. Yes, yes, there was a man, but it was not Stingaree. I saw him myself through coming up early, but I let him go as he had come, to save a fuss.'

'Through the window?'

'I am so ashamed!'

'Not a bit, Miss Bouverie. I am ashamed of bothering you. Confound the police!'

When the voices and steps had died away, Hilda Bouverie turned to Stingaree, her whole face shining, her deep blue eyes alight.

'There!' said she. 'Could you have done that better yourself?'

'Not half so well.'

'And you thought I could forget!'

'I thought nothing. I only came to you in my scrape.'

After years of imprisonment he could speak of this life-and-death hazard as a scrape! She looked at him with admiring eyes; her

269

personal triumph had put an end to her indignation.

'My poor Lea! I wonder how much she has heard? I shall have to tell her nearly all; she can wait for me at Melbourne or Adelaide, and I can pick her up on my voyage home. It will be no joke without her until then. I give her up for your sake!'

Stingaree hung his head. He was a changed man.

'And I,' he said grimly — not pathetically — 'and I am a convict who escaped by violence this afternoon.'

Hilda smiled.

'I met Mr. Brady the other day,' she said, 'and I heard of him to-night. He is not going to die!'

He stared at her unscrupulous radiance.

'Do you wonder at me?' she said. 'Did you never hear that musical people had no morals?'

And her smile bewitched him more and more.

'It explains us both!' declared Miss Bouverie. 'But do you know what I have kept all these years?' she went on. 'Do you know what has been my mascot, what I have had about me whenever I have sung in public, since and including that time at Yallarook? Can't you guess?'

He could not. She turned her back, he heard some gussets give, and the next moment she was holding a strange trophy in both hands.

It was a tiny silken bandolier, containing six revolver cartridges, with bullet and cap intact.

'Can't you guess now?' she gloried.

'No. I never missed them; they are not like any I ever had.'

'Don't you remember the man who chased you out and misfired at you six times? He was the overseer on the station; his name may come back to me, but his face I shall never forget. He had a revolver in his pocket, but he dared not lower a hand. I took it out of his pocket and was to hand it up to him when I got the chance. Until then I was to keep it under my shawl. That was when I managed to unload every chamber. These are the cartridges I took out, and they have been my mascot ever since.'

She looked years younger than she had seemed even singing in the Town Hall; but the lines deepened on the bushranger's face, and he stepped back from her a pace.

'So you saved my life,' he said. 'You had saved my life all the time. And yet I came to ask you to do as much for me as I had done for you!'

He turned away; his hands were clenched behind his back.

'I will do more,' she cried, 'if more could be done by one person for another. Here are jewels.' She stripped her neck of its rope of pearls. 'And here are notes.' She dived into a bureau and thrust a handful upon him. 'With these alone you should be able to get to England or America; and if you want more when you get there, write to Hilda Bouverie! As long as she has any, there will be some for you!'

Tears filled her eyes. The simplicity of her girlhood had come back to the seasoned woman of the world, at once spoiled and satiated with success. This was the other side of the artistic temperament which had enslaved her soul. She would swing from one extreme of wounded and vindictive vanity to this length of lawless nobility; now she could think of none but self, and now not of herself at all. Stingaree glanced toward the window.

'I can't go yet, I'm afraid.'

'You sha'n't! Why should you?'

'But I still fear they may not be satisfied downstairs. I am ashamed to ask it — but will you do one little thing more for me?'

'Name it!'

'It is only to make assurance doubly sure. Go downstairs and let them see you; tell them more details, if you like. Go down as you are, and say that without your maid you could not find anything else to put on. I promise not to vanish with everything in your absence.'

'You do promise?'

'On my — liberty!'

She looked in his face with a very wistful sweetness.

'If they were to find me out,' she said, 'I wonder how many years they would give *me*? I neither know nor care; it would be worth a few. I thought I had lived since I saw you last . . . but this is the best fun I have ever had . . . since Yallarook!'

She stood for a moment before opening the door that he unlocked for her, stood before him in all her flushed and brilliant radiance, and blew a kiss to him before she went.

The Governor was easily found. He was grieved at her troubling to descend at such an hour, and did not detain her five minutes in all. He thought she was in a fever, but that the fever became her beyond belief. Reassured on every point, Miss Bouverie was back in her room but a very few minutes after she had left it.

It was empty. She searched all over, first behind the curtains, then between the pedestals of the bureau, but Stingaree was nowhere in the room, and the bedroom door was still locked. It was a second look behind the curtains that revealed an open window and the scratch of a boot upon the white enamel. It was no breakneck drop into the shrubs.

So he had gone without a word, but also without breaking his word; for, with wet eyes and a white face, between anger and admiration, Hilda Bouverie had already discovered her bundle of notes and her rope of pearls.

There are no more tales of Stingaree; tongue never answered to the name again, nor was face ever recognized as his. He may have died that night; it is not very likely, since the young married man in the well-appointed bungalow, which had been broken into earlier in the day, missed a suit of clothes indeed, but not his evening clothes, which were found hung up neatly where he had left them; and it is regrettable to add that his opera-glasses were not the only article of a marketable character which could never be found on his return. There is none the less reason to believe that this was the last professional incident in one of the most incredible criminal careers of which there is any record in Australia. Whether he be dead or alive, back in the old country or still in the new, or, what is less likely, in prison under some other name, the gratifying fact remains that neither in Australia nor elsewhere has there been a second series of crimes bearing the stamp of Stingaree.